New Fiction

A Bridge Above Water

Edited by

Heather Killingray

First published in Great Britain in 2001 by
NEW FICTION
Remus House,
Coltsfoot Drive,
Peterborough, PE2 9JX
Telephone (01733) 898101
Fax (01733) 313524

SB ISBN 1 85929 035 3

FOREWORD

When 'New Fiction' ceased publishing there was much wailing and gnashing of teeth, the showcase for the short story had offered an opportunity for practitioners of the craft to demonstrate their talent.

Phoenix-like from the ashes. 'New Fiction' has risen with the sole purpose of bringing forth new and exciting short stories from new and exciting writers.

The art of the short story writer has been practised from ancient days, with many gifted writers producing small, but hauntingly memorable stories that linger in the imagination.

I believe this selection of stories will leave echoes in your mind for many days. Read on and enjoy the pleasure of that most perfect form of literature, the short story.

Parvus Est Bellus.

Contents

Countdown

Christine Williams

He counted everything, had done for as long as he could remember. All the verticals in the school railings, all the white ceramic tiles behind the boys' urinals. The steps to the office door. He counted the steps his bride took as she walked down the isle and then he counted the stained glass panels in the altar window.

He counted the stairs in a morning and checked them in the evening. He counted the Wheaty Squares in his cereal bowl, the number never varied; and then he counted the repeat pattern of fruit on the kitchen wallpaper. His counting had become second nature to him; he'd been doing it for so long. He looked on counting as a mental exercise. If he had to side-step someone whilst going for his bus he knew it would give him just two more steps. Rarely did his numbers alter. This gave him a lot of reassurance.

Numbers never answered you back or went through adolescent phases, unlike his children. Numbers never cheated on you either, unlike his wife, she said it was his fault and blamed his counting for her betrayals. 'It won't happen again' she would say; he had counted that three times up to now.

He had worked for the same firm for twenty-two years and climbed the same five steps, never four or six always five. Thirteen strides took him to his office door. He had over the years risen from office junior to senior payroll administrator. Four steps to his coat stand and six to his desk. Here he spent every working day checking numbers with absolute accuracy. Sometimes to have a rest from the ledgers he would gaze out of the four paned window and count the windows of the property across the way and as a special mental exercise he would count its vertical railings. Vertical lines at a distance had a habit of merging together but eventually he had mastered it.

This day he sat in his office counting the verticals on the railings and thinking to himself, 'do other people count things?' He thought they probably did, after all it gave a certain order to life. His wife said she didn't count things unless she had a definite need to know, but he didn't believe her, she only said it to try and stop him counting but it wouldn't work, she wasn't going to undermine him. He knew she lied because everyone counted things. His children said they didn't count things, that it was a stupid thing to do and that he should get a life. He knew they only said that because they were going through an adolescent rebellious stage and when they grew up they would acknowledge their need to count. He had never stopped counting through his adolescence; he had counted cars on the big dipper and seagulls at Bognor. He had even counted the legs of the dancers on Top Of The Pops but he reasoned that times had changed and when he was young there wasn't as much rebellion about.

One hundred and thirty-five. No! That wasn't right, he would have to count the verticals in the railings again. He did so three times but he couldn't get the right number, it had to be one hundred and thirty-two, nothing else would do. Perhaps he needed his eyes testing. He reasoned that the railings were across the road and it was raining which could have distorted his vision through the wet glass. He would count them again tomorrow, now he had work to finish before home time.

Six steps to the coat stand, four to the door, thirteen strides down the corridor and then down the five steps to the pavement. He liked those five steps. They were solid and dependable like his counting. He started towards the bus stop, ahead he saw a middle-aged lady walking towards him pulling a shopping bag on wheels. As she got closer she looked up, he side-stepped to his right, she side-stepped to her left, he side-stepped to his left and she stepped back to her right. It felt like some dreadful comedy that kept you watching but wasn't funny. He stepped back again and so did she, he stood his ground and she walked around him, now he didn't know how many steps he had taken. He looked back to the office and was about to return to the steps to begin counting again when he saw his bus coming. He turned to look at the bus stop and then back to the office steps, the bus was very close now and he knew he had to catch it or have a very wet wait for the next one. He gave one more glance at the distant office steps before running for the bus.

He told his wife about the woman but she seemed to miss the point, all she could say was, as least he hadn't missed the bus, she failed to see the importance of the uncounted steps. The children laughed and said he was lucky to have got away with both shins intact, that ladies with shopping bags on wheels were lethal. Lucky! He didn't feel lucky; he had failed to keep count.

He spent an unsettled night and woke early, as the light began to chase the shadows from the room. He lay next to his wife and waited for the alarm to ring. He counted the spots on the curtains and then the cracks in the ceiling. After that he counted the knots in the wardrobe doors. By the time the alarm rang he felt better. His wife went downstairs to begin breakfast and he used the bathroom. As he washed and shaved he counted the tiles behind the basin. He counted the stairs on his way down to breakfast.

He sat at the table and looked down into his cereal bowl. He could not believe this was happening; he always had three Wheaty squares. As he looked down he could see four. He took one out and put it back in the box, he always had three, no more, no less. He caught his wife looking at him; he knew she was doing it to annoy him. She raised an eyebrow and then turned back to the kettle, she didn't say anything, neither did he. He wondered why she was doing it, always three, no more, no less. She wondered why he only wanted two Wheaty squares that morning.

He left home and was feeling more relaxed as he reached the bus stop in the correct number of steps. When he got off the bus he was determined nothing was going to make him lose count today. He climbed the five steps to the main door. He liked those five steps, so solid, so correct. Through the door and thirteen steps brought him outside his office. Yes, he felt better.

Four steps to his coat stand and seven to his desk. No! No that wasn't right, he went back to the coat stand and turned. Carefully he walked back to his desk, four, five, six, seven, his desk was six steps. His ears began to pound; his breathing was harsh.

Clare knocked and walked in with his coffee, she stopped and watched him pace slowly and then he turned towards her. She wondered if he was unwell, his face was flushed and sweaty. He shouted, she had never heard him raise his voice before, he accused the cleaners of moving his desk. She look at the desk; it was large and heavy. She looked at its large feet. The desk had not been moved; it would have left indents in the flooring.

He started to ask her if she would walk from the coat stand to the desk but he found himself trailing off and accepting the proffered coffee. He had to accept the facts. He stared at the coat stand. Slowly it dawned on him, it was obviously the stand that had been moved and not the desk. He felt waves of relief flow over him as he counted from his desk and placed the stand in the correct place. He made a mental note to move the picture on the wall, he hadn't realised the stand covered it.

He sat behind his desk, he would do two hours work and then he would count the verticals across the road. As he worked the image of his father appeared in his mind's eye. He had been dead for five years and he still felt sad when he thought of him. It was his father that had started his counting. He would hold his father's hand as a small child and together they would count the stairs on the way up to bed. Then he would tell him counting rhymes. That had been fun but mostly there would be a serious reason for counting. Counting how many times he chewed his food to aid digestion. Counting the brush strokes to keep his teeth clean. His father had taught him counting was mostly a serious business.

At a knock on the door he looked up to see his boss walking in with a folder. His boss told him there was a mistake in the payroll. He didn't make mistakes, not with numbers. He took the folder and opened it. Neat numbers looked back at him. He checked the figures. He rechecked them twice; he loosened his collar and wiped his forehead. He kept checking and every time he got a different number. He looked out of the window and began counting the verticals. He counted and recounted them, why was the number wrong? He began counting again, his mouth felt dry. A lorry pulled up in front of the railings, he couldn't finish counting them. He jumped up from the desk; the folder fell scattering the papers. He staggered to the stand to get his coat, five steps, that was because he had moved it, why had he done that? He rushed down the corridor to the front door, forgetting to count the strides, he had to get outside, he needed to get some fresh air and count the steps on the way down, he liked those five steps.

His wife had a phone call asking her to go to the office; her husband was unwell. She had not expected to find him outside. He was shouting at people that there had to be five. He wouldn't let them near him, if they tried; he flailed his arms in the air. She had stood and watched as he had walked up and down the steps. Then he began to run up and down and she thought he would either fall or collapse. She tried to talk to him but he wouldn't listen, he said it was her fault; he accused her of moving the steps. She had called for their doctor, he had called for an ambulance, and her husband kept running up and down the steps counting. Just before the ambulance arrived he did stumble and two men grabbed and restrained him. He cried like a baby because they had taken him away from the steps and he needed to count them.

The doctors in the hospital spoke to him and then to his wife. They suggested he should go into a mental unit. She had agreed and visited him weekly. He'd been moved from the main ward, it was considered too full of countable objects. He was now in a very nice room on his own. He felt much better, he knew if he could get the numbers right he'd have order again. He counted and recounted everything in his room and always got the same number. Yes he had order, but he counted everything again just to be sure. One table, one chair, one bed. He smiled, numbers were so reliable.

HORCH

Seãn Jackson

Horch had his rock.

Now, you and I may well have a secret place to which we go when we're tired, fed up, or when we just need to be quiet and think. I knew a rugby-player once - a great beer-swilling bull of a man he was, all farts and fornication - he had a bench in the Country Park which he used when he was miserable or confused; when he had to get away from whatever his wife had prepared for his trouble. Many of us have such a place. Some keep it secret, and some don't.

Horch had his moments, and noisy wild hilarious moments they were. He was a great joker - not in any way that would cause anyone any harm, but mischievous nonetheless. But for all his good humour, there were times when something inside him made him feel he simply had to get away. And at times like this, Horch made for his rock and rested.

So it was, one century, that Horch was relaxing there. He had approached deep in thought and silently. It was only after he had been there for some time that he took any notice of his surroundings: And became aware of soft sounds.

Carefully looking to the base of the rock, he saw there a woman dressed all in black. It was not the black that he stared at; but her features, her form, her shape. She was not beautiful in the way that you or I might use the word. Not ordinarily pretty, fine-featured, photogenic or whatever; hers was a real out-of-this-world beauty of the fantastic sort that makes your heart feel instantly that it has become two sizes larger than will fit inside your chest. Her looks would stir the loins of every man and the envy of every woman; looks to make a dragon drool.

Petra, for that was the name of this vision of loveliness, felt water on her cheek and wondered at her tears. She was sad, certainly, she knew that. But hers was a deep melancholy rather than a crying misery. She opened her eyes at the instant another drop landed, too warm for rain. She looked up and saw Horch's great mouth, and was terrified. Her fear held her rigid on the lush soft grass, when all she wanted to do was run away.

Horch had one hell of a job comforting her and assuring her that the business of Dragons eating maidens was a load of old nonsense. She in turn pointed out that she wasn't a maiden anyway, and they both laughed. He singed her hair a little at this, and she giggled and made him promise to turn aside when he laughed in future.

They met often at the rock from then on, and had wonderful times. Their meeting spanned only a short while as far as Horch was concerned. For Petra, it meant most of her life. To both of them, their times at the rock became happy, laughing or thoughtful as their moods took them. On every occasion, each of them felt better, lighter, more contented and relaxed for having been there and having spent time together.

But we none of us last forever, you know. Horch witnessed Petra being interred from afar. He had no other contacts among the hue-mans. None of them would have bothered to understand him as Petra had done. He watched and grieved; and waited.

When everyone else had gone, and after night had fallen, he quietly dug up the grave and opened the ugly, clumsy box. He gently lifted his beautiful Petra, and holding her to him as he had done so often in play, re-closed the loose earth with his hind claws.

Then more gently than you or I would have dreamed possible, he carried her to their rock, and buried her beside it.

One or two of the hue-mans wept publicly for her in the cemetery for a few weeks, then forgot.

Horch cried alone for centuries; holding his rock, their rock. His grief had a certain strange secret happiness at its core.

It was called *love.*

* * * * * * *

(Ancient Romans, a civilised people by all accounts, got to know of this. They used the name Horch to signify 'quiet', and Petra as 'a rock'.)

Making A Mountain Out Of A Molehill

Stephen Hullyer

'This had better be good,' said Helen angrily. 'I've been waiting for nearly half an hour. What kept you?'

Simon felt the familiar tightening of the gut as he tried to justify his late arrival. He always had that feeling when faced with confrontation, especially if the person doing the asking was Helen.

'It wasn't my fault,' Simon said sheepishly, as he got out of the car to help Helen with the shopping. 'I was bang on time when this bus in front of me overturned and slid down the hill. Thanks to my razor sharp reflexes I was able to get off the road in time. Now, if I hadn't have reacted as I did, you wouldn't be getting a lift at all.'

'That is the biggest load of rubbish I have ever heard,' Helen snapped. 'You'd have thought a simple request like, 'Pick me up in half an hour,' would have been child's play, but no, you have to turn it into some sort of international disaster that only affects you. Isn't it weird how none of these strange occurrences are ever reported on the TV?'

Simon hung his head like a scolded schoolboy outside the Headmaster's office. He decided his best course of action was to put up the barricades and wait for the ferocious storm to pass. It normally did after a few days!

'Well, I'm fed up with your lies and cheap excuses,' she ranted, oblivious of Simon, who seemed to be shrinking with every passing minute. 'If you can't face me and give me a proper explanation then I think we'd better forget the whole thing!'

At this point Simon seemed to grow larger as if someone was pumping him up. 'Look, I'm really sorry,' he said in his best apologetic voice. 'Give me one more chance please. I promise it won't happen again.'

Helen glanced over at Simon and all her anger seemed to evaporate like a pool of water on a hot day.

'All right,' she said with a sigh, kicking herself for giving into his pleading puppy eyes. 'I'll give you one more chance and if you mess up, we're through.'

The following week, Helen was again outside the local supermarket.

'Now remember what I said,' she said to Simon, in her Primary School teacher's voice. She had to be like that, otherwise he'd never learn. 'You try and fob me off with some crummy excuse and we're history. Got it!'

Simon had 'got it'. He knew he had reached the last chance saloon and, if he messed up this time, he would have definitely blown any chance of them settling down together.

He watched as she wheeled the trolley through the doors before driving off. He hadn't gone far before he heard the sound of a siren. He pulled over and, like anyone with a morbid sense of curiosity, looked around to see which one of the emergency services, was in a hurry.

Suddenly the side door opened and a great ogre of a man got in, brandishing a lethal looking knife.

'Drive,' he said, almost snarling.

Simon didn't ask where and obeyed. He glanced over at the man and recognition sparked through him.

'Haven't I seen you before?' Simon asked, curiosity getting the better of his fear.

'Yeah, on TV most probably,' replied the man in a gruff voice. 'I'm famous, or I will be soon by the end of the day. I'm Ronald Matthews but most people call me . . . '

'. . . Christ!' Simon exclaimed, cutting in on Matthews, as the colour drained from his face. 'You're Ron 'Sweeney Todds' Matthews.'

Matthews glared at Simon with a stare that would have turned the Medusa to stone. 'Didn't your Ma ever tell ya it's rude to interrupt people when they're talking, especially me,' he yelled across the car, deafening Simon in one ear.

'Sorry,' Simon uttered timidly. 'Where do you want me to take you?' he asked, hoping a change in conversation would diffuse the tension.

'Just drive and cut the chat,' Matthews growled and lapsed into silence.

As they approached the railway crossing the automatic barriers began to descend, indicating that a train was approaching. On the other side they could see two police cars, their sirens wailing and their lights flashing.

'It looks like you'll have to turn yourself in,' Simon suggested hopefully.

Matthews turned to look at him and said, with a voice that would have made the dead restless, 'I'm not going back. They'll have to kill me first!'

A distant whistle sounded, making Simon jump. The train was getting nearer.

'Hit the gas,' Matthews ordered.

From what Simon had read in the news Matthews wasn't a man you argued with. He'd got his nickname of Sweeney Todds because of four different hairdressers. Convinced they had given him a bad haircut he'd cut their heads off and put them behind the shampoo bottles!

Simon 'hit the gas' and the car screeched forward, crashing into the automatic barriers. The impact tore off the roof and hurled it high into the air like a Majorette's baton.

As they sped by the startled police, Simon said, 'Look at my car. What will Helen say?'

Then he remembered Helen. Oh God. He was supposed to pick her up half an hour ago.

'Shut it,' bawled Matthews. 'Forget her. She'll come round when she sees your new convertible!' He burst into laughter at his own attempt at humour.

Simon felt that familiar tightening of his gut as a confrontation neared. Who cares if he's a mass murderer. He was fed up with people telling him this, people telling him that. He'd had enough. It was time to do something for himself.

A rage began to grow inside him like a kettle boiling. Slowly at first, and then when it reached boiling point, it exploded like an angry dragon.

'I've had quite enough of you,' Simon yelled. 'I've had it up to here with people nagging at me. If it isn't Helen moaning, then it's some escaped convict who's blown a gasket!'

Matthews glared over at Simon, who just glared back. He was so angry he couldn't see anything for a red mist. Ahead of them was a sign indicating the docks. Simon turned into the narrow road and when he saw the docks ahead, he floored the accelerator.

'What are you doing?' Matthews screamed out. 'You trying to kill us?'

'You said you weren't going back alive,' retorted Simon, as he pushed the accelerator to the floor.

'I - I was joking,' Matthews stammered with fear, as he tried to back away in his seat.

'Well here comes the punchline,' Simon said, as the car careered off the jetty into the dark waters below.

* * * * * * *

Simon sat drinking a cup of hot chocolate in the back of the ambulance. His hair was ringing wet and, with the red blanket wrapped around him, he looked like a radish.

One of the policemen, who had fished them out of the sinking car, walked over to him and said, 'Thanks to you, Matthews is pleading to come back. We owe you a huge debt. Is there anything we can do for you?'

'Yes there is,' Simon said thoughtfully, as he warmed his hands around the mug. 'Could you explain what happened today to Helen my girlfriend? I have a feeling she won't believe me!'

The King Of Hoi Polloi

Lee Jackson

Franklin told me once that we were all kings or queens. He said that no matter what our circumstances were that we'd always have something to rule over. I guess he meant our own lives.

Franklin had always been a little surreal and whimsical, yet nothing really signalled his inimitable demise into becoming a menace to society. None of the mother-hating, bed-wetting, animal torturing traits were there in his childhood - Franklin wasn't evil, just a little left of centre. He always wore normal clothes, no fads in black, no *faux* military garb. A jeans and T-shirt guy was Franklin. Jeans and T-shirt. How normal. How ordinary.

He told me once about how he had found this racoon in the park. Somehow, he said, he managed to coax it into his hands. Franklin always believed he had an affinity with animals. Dr Dolittle was his childhood idle. In his formative years he always wanted to be the great animal lover himself. He even found himself a top hat and tails at a car-boot sale and would put them on and parade around the local zoo, stopping at cages and holding conversations with the trapped animals. Alas he got more attention from people than the actual animals, but it never perturbed him. I don't think he really noticed. He was a happy-go-lucky young man. Nothing phased him. If something didn't go his way then he wouldn't sit back for a second and show any regret. His head was always full of ideas and he'd simply glide into the next performance that his mind would decide to stage.

Anyway, he told me this racoon had told him that its name was Richard. Richard the racoon. I guess alliteration has always been rife in the animal kingdom. Richard the racoon told Franklin that he was far from home and lost. Franklin told him not to worry because he'd take care of him. Franklin told me that he'd taken him home and from that day on, he'd allowed the racoon to share his bed. He shared his bed with Richard. I urged him not to mention too loudly in public that particular fact. I didn't believe him of course. You don't find racoons here - it was most likely a squirrel.

I guess I never saw the end coming for Franklin. I always imagined he'd be drifting across this world forever. Despite his strange little quirks he was an ordinary guy. Minus the Dr Dolittle raiment, he was ordinary. You could barely pick him out in a crowd. He'd be one of those ordinary faces that you wouldn't even realise you'd forgotten about. He was normal in so many ways.

It's just when he decided to take a lie down that morning that people started recognising him more. Franklin, being Franklin, didn't find a nice park bench to rest his weary legs. He chose the middle of the road. He just sprawled himself across the road, head and torso one side of the white line, legs on the other.

I guess it was lucky that the first drivers to come across him, did notice and managed to stop in time before crushing him. No one would move him. I guess people have bad impressions of others these days. He obviously looked disturbed enough, so it was best to leave him be. Eventually the traffic built up and drivers were getting irate. A policeman arrived on the scene and tried to converse with Franklin, but all Franklin would repeat was my name and address. So the authorities came and got me. I went to Franklin. A sizeable crowd had gathered around him, people were out of their cars and had come forward to see what the obstruction was. Shoppers lined the pavements and I got the impression that everything had stopped for Franklin. It was as if this was his own procession, his own street carnival, but no one was rejoicing. I knelt down beside him and he looked at me and smiled. I asked him what he was doing and he said he had found a new career as a sleeping policeman. What easier line of work could there be? I said that it was actually a dangerous and a very high risk line of work. He looked at me suddenly concerned. I told him that whilst he would be doing a great public service to the community, cars and lorries would be rolling over him. He sat up, a fearful look swept across his eyes. I added that Richard would be lonely. He nodded and looked at his hands as if for that second he held everyone's destiny in them. He asked me to stop for a second and think of what he had done. It seemed to suddenly dawn on him that he had made people late for appointments. There could have been a pregnant mother hurrying to hospital. He said he could be causing her pain. He could be making someone late for a flight. Important meetings would go unheard. He pulled his eyes away from his hands and looked at me. He looked deadly serious as he told me there could have been a nuclear technician hurrying on his way to avert a global disaster, sitting in his car getting frustrated. Franklin became worried that he would be responsible for the end of the world. I told him not to worry and that the world was fine and that there would only be a few burnt dinners on his head. I helped him up. He apologised and said that he felt like a tyrannical King for having made intrusive steps into all those people's lives.

But that was Franklin. The King of ordinary people.

The Mobile Phone

T G Bloodworth

They met as always on race days at their local ‘The Angel’. Usually they had one round, discussing form and expressing their thoughts on the forthcoming card. Always the same four, good friends over the years who worked hard, but always made time for a day at the Races.

John arrived first, swiftly followed by Michael and ‘Samson’. Samson was a nickname acquired at school, he stood head and shoulders above the rest. His real name was Claude but everybody, including his wife, called him Samson.

Bruce was late arriving and made his apologies. They all knew his wife Janet was very ill and needed treatment only available in the USA.

‘I’m sorry chaps’ said Bruce ‘but Janet needs me more today. She wanted me to go, but I said there will be other days.’
John said they understood, but did Bruce want a bet?
‘Funny thing’ said Bruce, ‘I woke up feeling lucky today, but first things first.’
‘I’ve got my mobile,’ said John, ‘give me a few pounds and ring me on the course, it’s no problem.’

Samson was driving, making good time, they arrived half an hour before the first race. On the journey up, conversation turned to Bruce and Janet, how they wished they could help, being such close friends.

For the moment the Races held their attention and John remembered to switch his mobile on, just in case. It was early March, a chilly wind was blowing across the course, but the usual business went on. The lads all placed their bets and watched the runners going down to the post.

Then John’s mobile rang, reception was not too good in the stands but apparently Bruce wanted £20 on ‘Going Nowhere’, a 33/1 long shot. John had no time for argument, but did confirm the name although the line was bad. To make things easy John placed the bet on the Tote, rather than fight his way to the bookies, counting himself lucky enough to get ‘On’.

‘Going Nowhere’, belied the odds and his name, coming home 5 lengths to the good. The Tote paid 70-1 for a win, but they all agreed it couldn’t happen to a nicer chap. As Bruce was very shrewd, John didn’t expect another call. With £1400 safely tucked away, the others played on with mixed success.

Just before the fourth race, John’s mobile rang again. It really was a terrible line, but Bruce’s tip was ‘Coaster’.
‘Put a £1000 on to win.’
John gasped ‘Don’t muck about, how much really?’
£1000 was confirmed, with little time to spare before the off, the three lads placed the bet between them. Most Bookies were offering 8 or 9-1 and seemed only too happy to take the bets.

‘Coaster’ did just that, coming up the final hill the lads were jumping out of their skins. As they collected, they realised that Bruce was something like £11,000 to the good. There were still three races to go, but John was becoming uneasy carrying all of Bruce’s winnings.

However, reassured by Samson’s presence, they decided to stay for two more races.

During the fifth race they had a drink, all excited about returning home and paying out Bruce. Then the mobile rang, in the bar reception was even worse, but it seemed that Bruce wanted a bet in the sixth race, another £1000 to win. Looking at the race card they could not believe the selection. ‘Home Sweet Home’, had form to match a selling plater. Checking the ‘Tote Approx Win Odds Board’, it showed 125-1 just then.

Hesitation and doubt took root, but Michael the coolest of the three was adamant.
‘It’s Bruce’s money and we must do what he says. If he loses, he’s still about ten grand in front.’
By now their own selections didn’t matter, so engrossed with Bruce’s request, it was off to the Tote.

The bet was placed, the approximate win odds shortened slightly to around 90-1. Up in the stands they found it difficult to concentrate, the size of the bet and the possible outcome.

'They're off' roared the tannoy and the crowd, John's hands shook so much, he put down his binoculars unable to watch.

The result was never in doubt, when the favourite fell three out, 'Home Sweet Home' was left in front. Jumping the last, he came up the hill to the Bookmaker's cheers at a returned price of 50-1.

All three marched to the Tote, it paid just over 80-1 for a win. They accepted a cheque on behalf of Bruce, for just over £80,000. Never in their wildest dreams had they enjoyed a day like this.

John with about £10,000 in cash and the cheque decided enough was enough.
'Let's get this money back to Bruce, he'll be waiting at The Angel about 8pm this evening.

None of the three seemed to know how they had personally fared, all the conversation was about Bruce and Janet and the amazing run of luck they'd had.

Arriving at 'The Angel' all excited, they found no sign of Bruce, then the landlord appeared.
'Hello lads,' terrible news for you to come back to.'
'What's on then Jim,' said Michael as always the coolest.
'Your mate Bruce left here just after you this morning, crossing the road he was knocked down by a lorry. The emergency services were quick in attending, but sadly Bruce died in the ambulance. I'm not sure what he meant, but just before he died, he said *Make sure Janet gets the money.*'

Her Ephemeral Ladyship

Rosemary Vandeldt

It was little Agnes Whiteley's birthday. A birthday was always something of an event in the Autumn Serenity Home - even so insignificant a birthday as the eighty-fifth, which fell fifteen years short of 'the big one'. There would be a sing-song, a special tea with a large cake and, of coursc, extra visits for the birthday lady. Little Agnes, however, had never, in all her years in the Serenity Home, had a visitor, or even so much as a Christmas card. She was a rather frail little creature who did not talk much about herself, or her past life, as most of the residents did, but it was well known (because Mavis Hawkins had lived in the same neighbourhood as Agnes) that some years ago Agnes had quarrelled bitterly with the daughter who was her only living relative. It was an unremarkable tale really, and an old one. The daughter had 'taken up' with an undesirable young man of whom Agnes had vociferously disapproved, a domestic altercation had resulted and the headstrong girl had stormed out of the house and out of her mother's life, if not her mind. All this had happened some time ago and as year followed year Agnes' health had visibly deteriorated and she had kept herself very much to herself. Birthdays had come with relentless frequency without any filial acknowledgement and Agnes would have ignored them too, but for Matron whose custom it was to haul to the front-stage the 'birthday girl'.

This year, however, things were different and the whole Home was agog. Out of the blue Agnes had received a letter - a week before her birthday - from the prodigal daughter herself, issuing an invitation for her mother to visit her at Chevingstone Hall at 11 o'clock on the morning of her birthday. The normally silent Agnes had fairly twittered for the last two days and now, in all her finery, she waited by the sitting room window for her 'conveyance'. Promptly it arrived - a chauffeur-driven Rolls Royce. Fussily escorted down the drive by Matron and most of her fellow residents, Agnes was saluted by the smartly uniformed chauffeur and settled in the back seat under soft rugs and away she purred to her incredible reunion.

Chevingstone Hall was a beautiful mansion set in acres of parkland with formal gardens, a lake and vast stable accommodation. Agnes gasped as

she was driven up the long driveway - (Mary's young man, whom she understood was 'away' at present, could not have been so bad after all)! An immaculately dressed butler admitted her to the house, took her coat and showed her into a large, elegant drawing room where her daughter, Mary, was waiting for her. The emotional reunion between mother and child swept away the long years of enmity and they chatted pleasantly (if a little shyly) over sherry served in sparkling crystal glasses. After a while Mary rang the bell and the immaculate butler appeared.
'McGarry.' said Mary airily, as if enjoying showing off to her humble parent, 'the children should be in from their ride now - would you call the Nursery and have them brought down? And tell Nanny I expect them to be on their best behaviour; their - er - grandmamma is here!'

If a little non-plussed by this unaccustomed aggrandisement, Agnes was, nonetheless, ecstatic. She had sat wistfully on the edge of 'boasting circles' in the home when photographs of grandchildren were passed round and had tried hard to smile admiringly like the rest. Now she would have something to tell them all! Her daughter had become a fine lady in a grand house with servants who showed her respect. Best of all, though - *she had grandchildren*! She need no longer sit awkwardly on the edge of the Autumn Serenity social circles!

Soon the door opened and a rosy-faced young nanny entered leading the children: a little girl with fair, pretty curls very like Mary's had been and a younger brother who resembled Agnes' late husband. (How proud he would have been today!) The generations greeted each other, a little awkwardly at first, but soon the natural friendliness of the youngsters came to the fore as they told her all about their rides on the 'horseys'. Their mother seemed a little tense as if she was afraid the children might say or do something wrong, but they were beautifully behaved.

It was not long before the butler made another appearance, this time to announce that 'luncheon would be served in the summer dining room' and the small family party followed him down a long, lushly-carpeted corridor. The awe-inspiring dining room looked out onto a rose garden. There were old portraits on the walls and the shining silver on the gleaming oak table was impressive to Agnes' blue, ageing eyes. The food was quite the finest she had ever tasted, served by maids in crackling white aprons. After the meal had ended Mary took her mother for a walk in the extensive grounds whilst the children returned to the nursery apartments for a rest. They were to join them later for tea in the drawing room, Mary said.

The children were brought down to the drawing room by the young nanny and they found their grandmother happy and rosy-cheeked. Tea was served, poured from a silver teapot into dainty china teacups and a special birthday cake was brought in for Agnes, exquisitely iced in pink and white and covered with edible rosebuds. After tea the children played games with their mother and grandmother and listened with interest as Agnes told them of her own life when she was a child. All too soon the butler arrived to announce that the chauffeur was waiting to convey Mrs Whiteley home. Once again, Agnes settled in the grand, comfortable car with a contented sigh. Mary had kissed her and promised to keep in touch. She had said nothing about return visits to The Hall, but assured her mother that she would bring the children to see her at least once a month.

Back at the Autumn Serenity Home Agnes was treated with new respect. The ladies never tired of hearing about her daughter's grand, ancestral mansion, the servants and the beautiful parklands.

It was fortunate that only *one* of the residents could remember reading, a few weeks back, that Mary Whiteley, a struggling single parent, had won a competition. The prize? A day (of her own choosing) as mistress of a stately home with full use of all its amenities and the service of its staff. Phyllis Baines was a kind woman and probably the only person in the home who could keep such knowledge to herself. She was pleased to see the new, sparkling Agnes happily reconciled with her family. She was also the only one who recognised the kindliness of fate when Agnes' health began to deteriorate further so that it was not necessary for Mary to think up excuses when she did not invite her mother back to Chevingstone Hall.

Gypsy Lady

Ken Jeffery

When his wife died Jack did nothing to change the cottage. A lady from the village came in to keep it tidy. Her husband did the same for the garden. It looked the same as the day she stood at the door before taking to her bed. Her bedroom was never slept in. He sensed the ghosts and they were pleased.

His spare time was spent walking. Mostly it was the Bratton Hills, where she had been so happy. The more he walked, the less he felt.

He became a familiar figure, head slightly bowed, as though engaged in deep thought. He always acknowledged a greeting or a comment on the weather.

Described by the locals as a loner. Their rustic philosophy was 'Better a loner than a gonner'. Ploughman's and cider for lunch, the landlords would set their clocks by him.

Many thought he should get a dog. Many kindly farmers offered to give him one. What with work, walking and tidying the grave, there was little time.

True it often crossed his mind. The fellow walkers, with the dog to heel, or children throwing sticks. The mutual delight of dog and child as with wagging tail the stick was returned to their feet. These were but jewels along the way. He must not be distracted. His walks, some said, were a pilgrimage. Tracing their steps perhaps?

Like most servicemen, he missed the comradeship. Reflected sadly on the youths, who aping the military in dress but not in mind. Attacking old women and the vulnerable were not in his creed.

The walks were not without incident. The bird wounded in flight, the sheep caught in the wire. The rabbit transfixed by the stoat. There on that springy turf of the chalk downs, the White Horse became a familiar friend. Nature was his agent and he understood Wainwright's philosophy. He was still a long way from discovering his own.

It was the threat of rain. The sun peered from behind a cloudy curtain, unsettled was the forecast. 'A bit like myself' he thought.

He decided on a local walk up the back lanes. Then the bus to the Bell. The cider still brewed on the premises. If it rained it would be a long, wet lunch in more ways than one. If it turned out fine, the soporific cider would do its stuff. What could be better than a nap in the Wiltshire sun and dream of their days together.

The Bell was small, untidy, no car park. The landlord serving direct from the wood. The barrels tipped on stands behind the bar. Lunch was as always bread, cheese and pickles. It was both large and fresh. The bread crusty, the local cheese too strong for mice, was the Landlord's boast. The pickles came from a huge jar. Not the marbles of the supermarket. They were the size of tennis balls. Left by his grandmother, so he said.

This was no theme park but an Inn. Two pints of the rough stuff was needed to quell the burning of these monsters. The Landlord knew his stuff. Drank his own ale and made you feel welcome.

There was a Snug somewhere, but it was never used. Here in the bar you could see, you could watch the drawing process. Each gleaming pint eyed by mine host. Then it was passed to the anxious customer by this paragon of the pub.

Around the walls were notices of collections for charity. Even the Distressed Gentlefolk got a mention. There were picnics for the lads and a nicpic for the ladies.

The cricket match, Gentlemen versus Farmers had been cancelled. The reason given, not enough Gentlemen. This was indeed a happy pub.

The onions acted as a deodoriser. The sawdust a reminder of trees and times past. To walk from sawdust to a country lane was a natural merging of events. Thick carpets and oily car parks do not merge in the same way. He buttoned up his windcheater. A sensible precaution after the onions and headed for the moors. Once the haunt of gypsies.

Against the wall of the Pill, lay the rusting boats, pinned like moths. He rested in the sun. The boats tilting at ungainly angles, waiting for high water. Then, like caterpillars, to spread their sails and regain their beauty.

He decided to get the bus back. It was a ride through the place names of Wiltshire, Upton Scudamore, Crockerton, Shear Cross and the Devrills.

All well-photographed, to be hung on some dusty city wall and shaken by the roar of increasing traffic. The bus would soon stop running. Why visit when it was on a calendar. There were direct buses to the new shopping malls. He felt the countryside was shedding her leaves in sheer relief.

The next day he decided to walk the local lanes. The long pull up the cut made him feel tired. Yesterday's cider perhaps? It was time to find a grassy bank. There on the verge was a caravan. The lane was secluded and his curiosity was aroused. The name of the original owner had been blacked-out by time and weather. It was a splendid affair reeking of times past. The wooden wheels and solid tyres gave the van a look of obstinacy, it would not be easily moved. It was happy where it was.

It was an isolated spot. Not everyone would have decided to live here. He approached from the back of the van. That it was occupied there could be no doubt. Paraphrasing the popular television show. He thought 'Who would live in a house like that'?

He was soon to find out and it was with a feeling of excitement he got closer to his unexpected find.

From the cast-iron chimney smoke belched even in the warmth of summer. On the steps sat a lady, half gypsy, half funfair attendant. She was dressed in a black skirt and shapeless jumper smoking a clay pipe, in tune it seemed with chimney.
'Afternoon,' the pipe never moved. Jack nodded. As a non-smoker he was interested in this piece of practised ventriloquism. A talking pipe.
'Afternoon,' he replied 'nice in the sun.'
The pipe remained steady.
'Always nice m'dear when you have no maister.'
They were both lonely, she for the open road, he for the stories, she would tell. When her travelling days were over, she bought the van, now she and it 'were laid up'.

The council, wise with Wiltshire wisdom, had decided she would be no problem. There she could see out her days. Jack was invited inside. That is the privilege of the wanderer.

Inside there was plenty of room, the brass shone and it was a 'little palace'.
'Do all me smoking on the steps rain or shine,' her laugh was musical.
'Saves a lot of baccy when it's snowing. You see mother would not have smoking indoors. As I will soon be joining her, it pays to respect her wishes.'
'Got an old wind-up gramophone, all her old tunes,' she laughed again.
'Sit on the steps and listen, be careful of the splinters.'
She went inside, scratchy but audible he heard 'When I grow too old to dream'. She sat down beside him.
'My mother sang that round the pubs, she had a good voice. Drink it was. My daughter did better, another good voice, made some records.'
She lit the pipe.
'Never see her now. What's worse, drink or fame? That's why I'm here, happiness and a bit of baccy.'

After that, Jack stopped many times for his fill of caravan philosophy. She never told him her name or mentioned her daughter, but he knew who she was and wondered how she felt if at all about her mother. Often he called before the pub and became so interested in her life story, he never made it for his lunch. When he listened to the tunes and her smoke-wreathed tales.

It happens to us all of course. Sadly smoke no longer came from the chimney and the steps had been taken away. His enquiries led him to the local farmer.
'They said she knew her time had come. She lit her pipe, walked to the nearest tree, sat against the trunk and died. When they found her the baccy was still warm. The stem of the pipe unbroken.'
The farmer was thoughtful, 'She left the caravan to her daughter, someone famous. It won't be collected, go for scrap I shouldn't wonder.'

He missed the Gypsy Lady. Only the walking could wipe away the tension. His wife's favourite had been the Limpley Stoke Valley, he would go there.

The sun was with him as he paused to look back on the lovely valley. Road, river and rail, topped by the viaduct and the canal. The long boats, now for pleasure only, creased the high waters.

There was a diesel. His imagination conjured a plume of smoke, he remembered his school days when engines were iron horses. Alive with steam, puffing their songs of power.

The diesels were dirty, spitting and yammering, like dying horses protesting every inch of the way.

Even the leaves fell from the bowed branches of the trees. Falling into the river, causing tear-like circles. Were they ashamed, at this so-called progress? He thought so.

Although he had not planned it he saw the Bath bus and decided to round off the day. The glass in the bus shut him off from the sounds of the country.

But the season's palette was still impressive. Today was Turner Day. Shadowy trees, misty rivers, the sun lightly dusting the hills.

In the valley the veiled bridges were pointing their buttresses at the water, which in gratitude, reflected their grace in ever-changing images, each one more beautiful than the last.

Jack sighed. The weir was wrapping itself around the City, like a tender mother, fearing the floods she had been created to protect. The park was still asleep. The deckchairs with their canvas stripes, were like sleeping citizens, lulled by the sound of the weir. By God it was beautiful. His wife would have loved that day.

The yellowing grass marking the site of the caravan turned green. Was it his imagination? When the stubble burned, he thought some of the smoke came from the foot of the tree where she died.

He still heard her songs from those who were rich and famous. When he shed a tear people told him 'It's only a song'. Jack knew better.

He never went to the daughter's concerts. He was content to listen to the reedy records. Remember her stories. Better than any book and to admire her independence. Superior always to fatuous fame.

He also remembered his wife's wishes. When they walked together she often said 'I love walking - we would be happy if we were gypsies.'

Special Treat

Geoffrey D Jenkins

Marigold Proctor was upset.

She had been upset ever since she had noticed the fast-approaching date on her 'Moggy Chunks' calendar in the kitchen. (A *Free* calendar with every 25 labels from the large-size tin). The date which seemed to leap out at her, inducing feelings of panic, was the most horrible, the most vile day in Marigold's year.

She took another peep through half-closed eyes, hoping desperately that she was mistaken. But no, the date remained obstinately the same.

'Oh well,' she murmured, 'can't be helped. I've a day or two yet, anyway.' She sighed and put the kettle on the old-fashioned stove. She was going to have a nice cup of herbal tea. Something to brace her up and stop her hands from shaking so.

Marigold jumped with fright as something warm and soft suddenly wrapped itself around her right ankle. For a moment she almost screamed, but then recognition transformed the unborn sound to a wheezy whisper. 'Jasper, you horror, you almost gave me heart failure!' She scolded the large, black tomcat half-heartedly as he continued to rub against his mistress's leg, purring loudly and looking up at her with two huge, amber eyes. Marigold bent down to stroke the sleek cat behind the ears. 'Daft old devil!' She straightened up slowly, Marigold was not a young woman anymore, she had notched up quite a tally on the score sheet of life. She was also very large boned. (That's what she told herself, anyway). The fact that she had recently thrown out the bathroom scales, because they had stuck on 20 stone, was neither here nor there. Those bones of hers did ache though, especially her back, as she finally regained a vertical posture.

She poured the boiling water from the kettle over the herbal sachet in her teapot. While it infused, she sat at the kitchen table and began to think . . .

Two days later, the October morning dawned dank and chilly. While the watery sun tried desperately to find a way through the grey blanket of cloud, Marigold was already busy in her kitchen.

She mixed ingredients, stirred, kneaded, poured, baked, cut and decorated, while thinking about the little monsters who would be the beneficiaries of her labours.

Every year she slaved over her stove to produce the beautiful and delicious biscuits, cakes and candies that she gave the children as treats. Even though, each year these were consumed with relish, she was still the victim of their annual tricks.

Each year, on the 31st October - Hallowe'en, the local children came to torment her. Not just her, of course. All the other folk living in the surrounding streets suffered the same fate. Well, not quite the same. Marigold did feel that she had been rather singled out for special attention.

Last year, a rotten fish through the letterbox. The year before, the front of the house flour-bombed and before that, dog excrement, sprinkled liberally over her lawn. Marigold had had enough!
'They will get something extra this year,' she said to herself, as she finished decorating the last delicacy with a flourish. Then her chubby fingers daintily selected a green marzipan dragon, with chocolate eyes, from the tray and popped it into her mouth.

With eyes squeezed tightly shut, she focused on the exquisite flavour. The dragon was quickly followed by a white chocolate ghost, a red marzipan devil and a cinnamon bat biscuit. Her fingers hovered again over the wonderful shapes, undecided.
'No, that's quite enough Marigold!' she chided herself softly.
'We'll need them tonight!'

Later that evening, soon after dark, the sounds of door knockers being knocked and doorbells being rung came to Marigold as she dozed in her fireside chair. She could hear the excited voices of children mixed with howlings, hootings and growlings as they acted out their characters, very vocally. Then they were coming through her gate, up the path to the front door. Her goats-head door knocker was banged heavily a couple of times. She could hear whispering.

Marigold got heavily up, picked up the two large trays from the kitchen and with great difficulty and heart beating furiously, opened the front door.

‘Trick or Treat! Trick or Treat!’ This ear-piercing cry came from a gathering made up of: one vampire, a werewolf, a mummy, three witches and a small, red demon.

Marigold held out the trays of goodies, forcing herself to say ‘Here you are my dears!’ Multicoloured hands reached out, grabbing at the treats and then, mouths started to munch happily. Marigold waited until the trays had been emptied. Then she said sweetly, ‘Wait here kids, I have a special treat for you this year. I’ll be back in a jiffy!’
And she closed the front door.

Marigold climbed the stairs to her bedroom. Once there, she changed into the old, black woollen cape that had originally been owned by an ancestor of hers, executed for witchcraft in 1633. She then carefully, with both hands, reached under her chin and proceeded to remove her mask. The latex mask that she had to wear at all times to cover the hideous disfigurement of her features.

Burned in a fire, long ago, there was not much left of Marigold’s face. Everything had melted together. Merged. ‘Thith thould do the twick,’ she lisped. Without the support of the latex it was difficult to enunciate clearly.

Marigold hurried back downstairs and stood for a moment behind the front door. Then, shrieking, ‘Twick or Tweet!’ at the top of her voice, she flung open the door.
Surprise but no shock.
Slight concern but no panic.
Then, ‘Ace costume!’ said the vampire.
‘Cool mask Miss Proctor!’ exclaimed an awed-sounding werewolf.
‘Yeah, brill!’ squeaked the little demon.
Then the whole group turned and scampered off into the night, laughing and making monster noises.

Marigold closed the door. Her shoulders slumped. They hadn't been petrified. They hadn't even been shocked. No nightmares for them. It hadn't worked? But there were no nasty pranks that night.

No fish. No flour. No excrement.

The kids had loved her trick.

Marigold was *wicked!*

THE SOLDIER'S CAP
Catherine Mair

Tom found the black beret in one of the children's boxes. When he put it on it looked incongruous with his black woollen singlet and work boots. He held his big hand in front of his chest and focused on his head and the beret. Yes!

Marianne was coming this morning to pack up the last of her gear and take most of the children's clothes and toys. The place was a mess. Her garden was overgrown with long grass and weeds and the cottage in which their fourth child had been born three years ago hadn't seen a clean up since the girls left with their mother.

At times the pain in Tom's chest made him wonder whether he was a candidate for an early heart attack. It felt like that this morning. When he turned from the shambles in the front yard he caught sight of himself in one of the cottage's dirty windows. Change. A new vision for the future. He went inside, took off the black singlet and work boots and rummaged through another of the boxes.

When Tom walked out into the yard again he looked wonderfully bohemian. His shirt was a colourful patchwork creation and instead of the greasy, old work shorts he usually wore, he was wearing purple shorts with multiple pockets. The black beret looked exactly right. He walked beneath one of the enormous Norfolk pines which loomed above the cottage and said in a strangely changed voice:
'I hate it when people see what I'm really feeling.'
Tom reached for one of the lower branches of the huge tree and hauled himself up. Limb by limb he dragged himself higher and higher until like a very colourful bird he perched near the top. As he gazed out over the beautiful countryside he felt an incomprehensible stirring, the urge to paint a *picture*. He felt dimly that a picture could be something other than a beautiful landscape or a picturesque scene. Tom loved colour. As he climbed down he could feel a fizzing inside his mind.

When Marianne drove hesitantly up the rough metal drive she couldn't believe her eyes. She was expecting to find a moody, sad man. Who was this exotic stranger? Tom walked towards her and said in a deep, accented voice:

'Good morning my dear. Would you like some refreshment? Lemon tea or iced coffee?'
'You're kidding! Iced coffee, since when. Well if it's for real, I could go an iced coffee.'
After their drinks Tom and Marianne got down to work. They dragged the cardboard boxes into the middle of the room and surveyed the remaining possessions.
'Jeez, (said Tom in a more Tom-like voice) look at this. It's a bit chipped. Probably the last one left after that row when you threw those plates. I know. I asked for a lot of it. Just as well I wasn't firing them at you. I'm a better shot. What a hell of a mess we've made though Marianne. What a bloody mess!'
'Remember me in this Tom. You used to chase me around the kitchen table growling, far out, I couldn't stop laughing.'
'I think Jimmy will still need these don't you Marianne?'
'Here's Sophie's money box. I wonder how many times we raided the kids money boxes when we were short of cash for the milk or bread?'
'What are we going to do about Rosie, Tom? She's looking old. She was amazing the way she'd hide her puppies down rabbit holes. What a job we had tracking her hiding place down.'
'Don't worry about the old girl. She's better out here on the orchard. I'll look after her.'
'I know Lucy will miss her Moon but I'm afraid it's better that the cats stay up here. They've been around for so long. They're too territorial.'

The last box was taped up and loaded into Marianne's van. The sun had gone down. It was cold.
'Au revoir,' Tom said doffing his beret. At least he wanted to appear nonchalant. Neither Tom nor Marianne wanted their tears to be seen.
On the bank near the drive Tom spotted a colourful patch of flowers, survivors from Marianne's garden.
'Wait a minute,' he called as he walked towards the bank. With his newly-focused artist's eye, he quickly selected a lovely posy.
'Good luck,' he said as he handed the flowers to Marianne.
Marianne had never been one for bright compliments but as she backed down the drive she called out:
'I like your beret.'

COURAGE

Lauren Murphy

It wasn't fear. It wasn't being afraid of something, that feeling of dread that everyone has experienced at one time or another in their lives.

It was more like a hard lump or bubble in the pit of your stomach and the bubble contained frustration, worry, anger and all the other emotions that I can't quite describe. When they provoked you, when they said something or sniggered or subtly gestured, they stuck a pin in the bubble and it burst. And each time it burst, the worry, anger and frustration spilled out and spread through your whole body like a kind of gluey syrup.

I don't deserve it. I know I don't. So why? Why me? I have asked myself that question so many times and I can never find an answer. *Never.* So, I don't bother asking it anymore and just accept things for the way that they are. But it doesn't stop the feeling I have, the awful feeling in my stomach.

I shouldn't care. I don't *want* to care what they think. I used to care a lot about what other people think of me, but not any more. That doesn't mean that it doesn't hurt when they say or do something. It's not always verbal. It's when they get through to your emotions, that's when it starts to hurt. It's not always direct. It can be a message passed on, a note scrawled on paper, a whisper behind a hand, a snigger here and there. Childish games. I have done it myself - I'll admit. Not to them, you understand, but I used to do it to other people. But when I realised how much it hurt to have it happen to you, I stopped. I learned to put myself in the other person's shoes and I stopped. Snide remarks and childish, petty, derogatory comments don't get you far. If only they could see and feel how bad it really is, this feeling.

Ignore them. How many times have I been told that? Ignore them and they'll see they're not getting to you. But they *are* getting to me, how can I make you see? They are. And I'm angry, so angry for letting it happen. Why should I let them? I have no respect for them because of what they are doing. I *should* ignore people who I have no respect for, so how do they provoke me?

I sat there one day. They were making trouble; I, and everyone else could see it and sense it. With their high-pitched squeals of laughter, like a coven of cackling witches. It may be a cliché, but the air was tense and the atmosphere was bad. I sat there, saying in my head over and over again, push me, push me, push me. Come on. Push me to the limit and see what happens. I don't know what would have happened. The feeling in my stomach was there. But they never pushed me. That's what they do; that's their game. I wonder if it's deliberate or not, the way they push you almost to the limit, when you're nearing boiling point, keep you on the brink, teetering on the edge. I wonder is there a thrill, a satisfaction in having power over someone, like Hitler and the Nazis? But they *don't* have power over me. That's the thing. They never will control me. I might be subdued, quiet, upset, worried, but they will never have control over me. Never. I refuse to let it happen.

Sometimes I blamed God. I asked for His help and He didn't give it. But it's wrong to blame Him,' He's not the one at fault.

How can I describe it? You can't describe it. It's impossible unless you yourself have gone through it, had the same bubble of anger and worry deep within your stomach, your being. And your head begins to ache; you don't want your lunch, so you put your head down to stay inconspicuous. It doesn't always work though. Sometimes, unless you're thinking really deeply, you can still hear their muffled voices go through your head.

But when you *do* get away from it, the relief. The comfort of having your friends and family around you, people who care about you and who you care about. And that's what keeps you going. It's like two different types of weather. When you're around them, it's bleak. The sky is blank; it's damp and windy outside. You want to find a safe, sheltered place. But when you're not near them, the sun is always shining and warm, there's a light breeze and you don't want the day to end.

One of my favourite quotes is 'Courage isn't freedom of fear; it's being afraid and going on'. I think I have courage, but I was never really afraid. Never.

Of Dreams And Angels

J Densham

' . . . and they lived happily ever after. Now it's time to put out the light.'

'Mummy, is it true? Do wishes really come true?'

Karen looked into the big, brown, innocent eyes, staring with such intensity and could not disillusion her.

'Oh yes. As long as you believe, then wishes come true.'

She brushed her lips against the warm forehead.

'I'm going to wish for a kitten.' said the four year-old decidedly.

'A ginger kitten with green eyes and a beautiful bushy tail.'

Karen bent forward to fold the bedclothes.

'Not too tight. I want to move my arms. Where's Snugget?'

'Here he is.' She placed the hand-knitted toy inside the sheet. Zoe smiled at it.

'And the glow lamp.'

'It's on.'

'I want Daddy.'

They played out the same ritual most evenings. Karen kissed her daughter again.

'He'll be home soon. I'll send him up to say goodnight when he comes in. Night-night.'

Zoe knew when she was defeated.

'Night-night.'

She lay in bed and made her wish and dreamed of ginger kittens when she slept.

Karen smiled gently and switched off the top light, but as she quietly closed the door, tears filled her eyes.

Do wishes come true?' She wondered as she went downstairs. 'I wish I could wake up and find it was all a bad dream - a mistake. Anything rather than this. Not a tumour. She's so young. Too little. Life hasn't started for her yet. Oh I wish with all my heart that Zoe could be well.

The key turned in the lock. As Alan opened the door tears were streaming down her face. He took her in his arms and she sobbed.

Now unbeknown to many (and understood by less), no thought, wish or prayer is ever missed or goes unanswered. In that eternal realm which some call 'heaven', the messenger angels, as usual, were about their work, eagerly fulfilling dreams and wishes. As soon as a thought fleeted its way into the ether it was lovingly caught by one of these ministering beings.

Shimra was new to her post and keen to do her best. So keen that she managed to catch both the child's and mother's wishes together. Protectively she carried them back to her mentor.

'Is it possible Areta?' she asked, 'can all prayers be answered?'
Areta, a very wise soul, had performed her task tirelessly for aeons, delighting in the fulfilment of each new desire; sharing the joy of the recipient and sometimes receiving thanks as a bonus. She looked at Shimra and chided gently:
'Trust, child. Prayers are always answered, although sometimes people do not realise it. Sometimes they are answered in a different way from what is expected. Yet they are always answered in the best way.
'What about these?'
Areta studied the wishes for a moment, then smiled tenderly at her young tutee.
'These seem straightforward. I don't foresee any major problems; just one or two little snags.'
'Can the brain tumour be cured?'
'Of course. Healing is easy, providing we get a good channel. We'll set up a network of links. Which churches are there in the area?'
'An Anglican; St Dominic's Roman Catholic; and a synagogue are the nearest,' said Shimra, consulting her information source, 'and there's a healing group.'
'Good. Now, let's see - Mrs Jones, Reverend Peters; Mrs O'Brien, Father O'Reilly; Mrs Stein, Rabbi Isaac; and . . .' she paused a moment, 'Mr Thomas. That should do it. No mosque?'
Shimra shook her head.
'Oh well. Can't have everything. That's the brain tumour sorted.'

'What about the kitten?'
'That's simple too. We just put a thought in the father's head and impress Eileen Simpson in Fielden Road to put a note in the local shop. She has a ginger kitten. It will fulfil her wish to find it a new home. Two in one there.' (There was just a trace of satisfaction in the tone).

'No. Our problem is the doctors.'
'The doctors?'
'Yes. Doctors are one of the most difficult groups to work with. They do like to rush into things. Once they've made up their minds it's very hard to get them to change.'
'What can we do?'
Areta considered. 'There is a way. Her mother will be a bit upset, but it will all turn out for the best. Right.
Let's get to work. It's Monday now, we only have a few days . . .'

The next day, Tuesday, Jan called round. Karen had been too upset to phone her best friend with the news. Jan read her expression and knew the test results were bad.
'The operation is on Friday. They have to shave her head. All her beautiful hair will be gone. There's only a twenty percent chance of recovery - but none at all if they don't operate . . .'
She began to cry.

Jan gave what little comfort she could, sharing the tears. Her eyes were puffy when she eventually left. She drove home via the supermarket and bumped into Mrs Jones, who was quick to notice the red eyes.
'Hello my dear. Is everything alright?'
'It's my friend's daughter, Zoe. She's got a brain tumour. Having it removed on Friday. She's only four. Such a lovely child. They don't think she'll live.'
'Oh my dear. I am so sorry.'
'I'm afraid I must go. Mark has a friend coming to tea and they'll be home soon.'
'Goodbye my dear. Take care.'
Mrs Jones was a caring lady, deeply troubled by what she had just heard. Her walk home took her past the vicarage, where Reverend Peters was watering his roses. He looked up.
'Hello Mrs Jones. Is anything the matter?'
'Oh Reverend Peters, I've just heard the most dreadful news. A child with a brain tumour, only four years old . . .'

Reverend Peters did what any good vicar would do. He put down his watering can and took her indoors for that proverbial British cure-all, a nice cup of tea. Half an hour later she left, with a lighter walk, having unburdened her sorrow to a compassionate ear; and Zoe's name was added to the list for healing prayers.

That same evening Mrs Jones shared a table with Mrs O'Brien and Mrs Stein at their flower-arranging class. As they set the chrysanthemums in place she told them about Zoe.
'For shame,' said Mrs O'Brien sadly, snipping her stalks. 'The poor little soul.
'And her parents,' agreed Mrs Stein, setting a flower in place and stepping back to survey the result. 'How her mother must be feeling.'

A cloud descended over them. All three went home that night deeply concerned about Zoe and her parents.

Every week the ladies on the committee of St Dominic's took it in turn to arrange the flowers. This Wednesday was Mrs O'Brien's turn. The plight of little Zoe still played on her mind as Father O'Reilly entered the church. Her eyes crinkled at the sight of her beloved parish priest, but he noticed a sadness about her. Relieved to share the worry, she told him of the illness.
'. . . and the poor child, just a baby. It's a sin so it is, a sin. How could God let it happen?'
'Indeed it might seem so, Mary' said the priest, kindly.
He had known Mary O'Brien since childhood and looked with compassion at the troubled face before him.
'It's not for us to question the will of God.'
But he added Zoe's name to the list for healing prayers.

That same Wednesday Mrs Stein was attending a coffee morning in aid of the old folks outing and found herself sitting next to Rabbi Isaac. The story of Zoe came out as she sipped her coffee and a tear spilled into her cup.
'We will pray for Zoe and her parents,' said Rabbi Isaac quietly, making a note of the name in his little pocket book.

Friday was looming ever closer.

Thursday arrived. Karen and Zoe had been shopping. Zoe clambered slowly out of the car clutching a fluffy toy kitten. A slight unsteadiness when she walked was the only outward sign of the tumour. Karen

carried bags to the door and stood, searching for her key. Zoe saw next door's cat across the road and ran to greet it. They were old friends.
'Here Pudsey, come and see my kitten.'
She tried to stop at the kerb but her legs gave way and she fell forward - Karen heard the screech of brakes and froze. Her brain screamed *Do something*, but she could not move. Like a slow-motion picture she watched the car driver kneeling beside her daughter. Then mercifully her body unlocked and she ran to the scene.

Zoe's frail little body lay in the road. She was pink and breathing quietly, with no obvious signs of injury. Just as if she was sleeping.

Neighbours also heard the noise and ran from their houses. One called an ambulance. Another rang Alan. In a daze Zoe and her mother were transported to casualty.

At work Greg Thomas took the call. He and Alan were good friends, having worked together for eight years. They shared lifts when one or other's wife had the car, like today. Greg belonged to a healing group where last evening they had prayed earnestly for Zoe's recovery. Now, as he drove Alan to hospital, he prayed again that she might survive this second disaster.

By the time they arrived in casualty Zoe was having a brain scan. Alan relived the nightmare, only this time he already knew the result. It seemed an eternity until he heard her trolley coming back to a cubicle. They waited. Zoe, now wide awake, looked round her partitioned enclosure.

The casualty officer came in smiling. Young, blonde, with a good figure and the confidence that came with knowing her job.
'The scan's fine - absolutely clear. There was no injury. We'll keep her in overnight just as a precaution. She can go home tomorrow.'
She beamed at Zoe, who stared back.
'It's okay, Mummy can stay with you.'
'What about the tumour?' asked Alan.
'What tumour?'
'Zoe has a brain tumour. She's having it removed on Friday.'
The casualty officer said 'Excuse me a moment,' and disappeared very rapidly. She quickly scanned Zoe's notes, then hurried to the main desk.

'Bleep Mr Harper, consultant neurologist. I need a second opinion. Fast.'

Mr Harper duly arrived and confirmed the scan was clear. He also confirmed the child was scheduled to have an apparently non-existent tumour removed on Friday. Tomorrow, in fact.
'There must be some mistake,' he muttered, searching for an explanation.
The consultant radiologist was called, the tests compared and results confirmed. The tumour had gone.
'I don't understand it.'
'I have heard of spontaneous remissions, but they're very, very rare.'
'Could it have been the steroids?'
'Never in my life . . .'
'It's a miracle.'

In the early afternoon of the Friday they had been dreading so much, Alan took them home. As they entered the house a little bundle of ginger-white fluff ran to greet them. Zoe's eyes lit up.
'A kitten! My very own, real kitten.'
She sat on the floor and the green-eyed kitten climbed on her lap. Karen looked at Alan.
'I thought she'd be safer with one inside the house. I saw a card in the paper shop. *Home wanted for kitten.* It was only in Fielden Road, so I called on my way home last night and collected it.

Zoe held the purring body in her arms.
'Mummy, wishes really do come true. This is the happiest day of my life.'
Karen laughed. Suddenly the scene in the bedroom last Monday flooded back. A ginger kitten.
Wishes do come true!
Her eyes filled with tears, but this time they were tears of gratitude.
'Oh thank you. Thank you.'
The words welled up from the depths of her being.

In the ether, Shimra and Areta together caught the thanks and laughed with sheer delight as they bathed in the warmth of love that surrounded them.

THE SENTRY

D R Walker

The Royal Airforce Regiment Sentry on the airfield at RAF Nicosia, Cyprus looked at his watch. Nearly 10.00am. He moved the position of his rifle which had been resting heavily on his shoulder for a considerable time; that's a bit more comfortable, he thought. He opened the flap on his khaki shirt and pulled out a packet of cigarettes, opened the packet and checked how many were left. Four, he noted. That's okay, only two hours left to go. He lit a cigarette and inhaled deeply. He looked towards his reason for sentry duty; twenty Cypriot men were repairing a portion of the tarmac, at the far end of the runway. They joked and laughed as they beavered away with pick axes, shovels. Hard to believe, the Sentry thought, that any of these men could be a EOKA guerrilla, capable of planting a bomb or in some other way causing damage to the RAF airfield. Anyway, they had to be watched.

A short time after, the workers all stopped what they were doing, made tea and began eating their lunch, whilst sitting around in a group talking idly.

The Sentry, who was about fifteen feet away, took his rifle from his shoulder and placed it against the wall of a small prefabricated shed which he was leaning against. That's a relief, he thought to himself. He noted that his khaki shirt had blue marks on it where the blanco had melted in the 90° temperature. He took a gulp of water from his canteen, wiped the sweat from his tanned face and put the rifle back on his shoulder. He could feel his exposed arms burning as the sun became even more fierce.

One of the Cypriots walked towards him 'Got a light Johnny?' (Almost every British Serviceman in Cyprus was called 'Johnny'). The Sentry obliged, pulling his cigarette lighter from his pocket and handing it to the dark-haired Cypriot. The man puffed on his cigarette until the end glowed red, all the while studying the Sentry's face.

'How old are you Johnny?' the Cypriot asked the Sentry.
'Eighteen,' came the reply.
'How long have you been in Cyprus?'

'Three months.' The Sentry kept an alert stance, as he watched the Cypriot warily.
'You like Cyprus?' the Cypriot asked.
The Sentry thought for a moment and then replied: 'Yes, I like it here very much. I like the sun, the swimming; Cyprus is a lovely island.' He cast his mind back to where he had lived just six months before. Cheltenham in England had been in the grip of a cold winter, with rain and snow making the days always seem bleak.
'Yes, I like it here very much,' he repeated, almost to himself.

The Cypriot interrupted the Sentry's thoughts.
'Why are all of you British troops here?'
The Sentry, who had read about the island before being posted there answered: 'Because Britain purchased the island from Turkey a long time ago and the British want to keep it.'
'You should all go back to your own country!' the Cypriot retorted bitterly, 'and let us have our island back. It is our country and of very little use to you.'
The Sentry looked back at the Cypriot and shrugged his shoulders.

The Cypriot changed the subject.
'Let's see your rifle Johnny,' he said, reaching for the Sentry's rifle, which was hanging from his shoulder.
'You cannot touch it!' came the Sentry's reply. The Cypriot ignored him and reached forward for the rifle sling.
'Get your hand off that sling!' the Sentry's voice was raised slightly.

The Cypriot ignored him and pulled at the sling even harder, causing the rifle to fall from the Sentry's shoulder.
The Sentry pulled the sling backwards and almost screamed at the Cypriot 'Let go, you idiot.'
A tug-of-war ensued, with the Cypriot pulling the sling and the Sentry pulling the rifle back towards him.

The other Cypriots, who had hitherto ignored the two men, stopped what they were doing and turned their attention to the apparent disturbance which now seemed to be developing.

Without warning, the Cypriot suddenly kicked his right leg with some force at the lower half of the Sentry's leg, but in so doing, he lost his grip on the sling. The Sentry was sent sprawling backwards and he too lost his grip on his rifle. The weapon crashed to the ground as the Sentry also stumbled and fell down onto the dry earth.

The Cypriot began laughing as the Sentry picked himself up and reached for his rifle. It was almost in his grasp when the Cypriot suddenly made a move towards him. The Sentry sensed danger and, without a second thought, he lashed out towards the Cypriot with some force with his fists. He caught the Cypriot square in the jaw and although this caused him to stumble backwards, the Cypriot managed to keep himself upright. The Cypriot, the Sentry guessed, was probably almost three stones heavier than he was and he certainly felt this when the Cypriot returned the attack and punched him in the chest and on the side of his head.

The audience of Cypriot workers gathered more closely around. Some began to either shout with excitement, or just watch in bemused silence.

The fight between the two men continued, each throwing punches and kicking the other in a bid to gain control of the other. Eventually, through sheer exhaustion, the fight stopped and the exhausted opponents faced each other, breathing heavily, glaring at the other; each wondering what the other's next move would be.

The Sentry knew he had to retrieve the rifle, which was lying a couple of yards away in the dirt. If he made a move towards it, he knew the Cypriot would be on him before he could pick it up.

The Sentry knew also that there would be no relief guard for at least an hour and this thought caused him to panic. He glared at the Cypriot, wondering what he could do. Suddenly, he remembered his bayonet, which he knew was attached to his belt. He quickly grasped the handle, pulled it from its sheath and held it threateningly in front of him.

At just that moment, the Cypriot had made a swift attempt to reach once again for the Sentry's rifle. The Sentry rushed forwards knocking the Cypriot off balance and they both tumbled to the ground. The Sentry stabbed at the Cypriot viciously and the bayonet went right through the middle of the Cypriot's hand, pinning his hand to the ground.

The Cypriot screamed in agony as the Sentry bent down to retrieve the bayonet, pulling the knife out expertly in one swift movement, causing blood to burst from the wound.

The Cypriot jumped up from the ground and clutching the wrist of his injured hand with his other hand, ran back towards the crowd of workers.

The Sentry picked up the rifle, dusted it off and fitted the bayonet back onto the barrel. Next, he expertly checked and prepared the gun for use and then re-hung it from his shoulder. He felt much safer now that he once again had control of his weapon.

The Sentry wiped the sweat from his brow and stood watching the group of Cypriots, unsure of what would happen next. A few minutes passed before three of the workers began to walk quickly towards him, stopping some ten feet away. The smallest of the trio addressed him in English: 'It was all just a joke that went too far,' he said hurriedly; 'please do not report the incident! Costasa is deeply sorry for what has happened. If he loses his job, his wife and family will suffer; he could end up in a detention camp!' The small Cypriot looked beseechingly at the Sentry, who stood with his arms folded across his chest.

As the small Cypriot spoke, the Sentry noticed that the man with whom he had been fighting - 'Costasa', he recalled he had been referred to - also began to approach the small group warily. His injured hand was now bound with cloth and he was smiling.

The Sentry regarded the man with distaste. Did the Cypriot really hate the British so much, or had it really been a joke which had gone too far? He knew that the Cypriot would indeed be in deep trouble if he decided to report the incident. The Sentry thought for a moment and then spoke. 'I will not report what has occurred here today, but none of you must tell anyone what has happened. If this incident is exposed, I will be in serious trouble for not reporting the matter.' He eyed them all suspiciously and then continued: 'I repeat that you must all keep quiet about this episode, or there will be trouble!'

The small English translator reiterated the conversation to the group, who all nodded and smiled emphatically. He turned back to the Sentry and extended his right hand 'You are a good man Johnny,' he said taking the Sentry's hand in his. The Sentry grinned and, casting a final look of warning at the group, he turned and walked away.

The Sentry chuckled to himself. So much for a peaceful day he thought! He tidied himself up and stood back on duty.

Some time later a large RAF truck appeared along the dusty road to collect the workers to take them back to Nicosia. As it drove away, Costasa waved cheekily to the Sentry and smiled smugly as the truck disappeared from view.

The Sentry stood for a few moments longer, smoking a cigarette and looking impatiently at his watch.

Soon, a Land Rover pulled up, driven by a member of the RAF regiment. A Sergeant accompanied him. The Sentry climbed in the back seat and exchanged pleasantries with the other occupants, as the vehicle picked up speed. The driver half turned round in the front seat and addressed the Sentry: 'Was everything OK today?'
The Sentry frowned back at him 'Why sure, why do you ask?'
'It hasn't been too good for some today,' the Sergeant continued; 'Two army lads were gunned down in Ledra Street.' Ledra Street was well known on the island as 'murder mile'. The driver chipped in with the news: 'All Cypriot workers have been ordered off British property until things calm down . . .'

The Land Rover sped faster along the bumpy road. The Sentry sat further back in the hot leather seat, patted his rifle and looked absently at the white rocks amongst the dry countryside on either side of the narrow tarmac road, as he reflected on how lucky he was to be alive.

STRANDED

Rod Trott

Standing alone, I was surrounded by two or three thousand faces. Everyone looking very shattered after spending hours and hours in a dirty, dreary carriage, shaking and rattling through this Sunday afternoon into the cold, black night.

Eventually this army of baggage carrying strangers all end up bleary eyed, hungry and wishing that they could be anywhere but here, here on Waterloo Station, killing time in the middle of a work to rule . . . courtesy of British Rail.

After the initial shock, I suddenly come to the realisation that there is no way that this is going to change tonight. Then all at once as if everybody seemed to have the same idea at the same time, there is a mad rush for the nearest phone and for the unlucky ones yet another wait.

'I'm sorry love, but there is no train tonight, so don't expect me home until tomorrow some time.' A few words of consolation and then alone again.

The thing to do now is to find a place out of the cold and wet, a place to rest those weary limbs. Some people are sitting on their cases, others have claimed a place on a bench, others are just walking around still wishing and hoping that a miracle will happen . . . these are the less experienced travellers, caught up in something there is just no sense in trying to understand.

These lonely hours can be very unnerving if you don't know what to expect. For these are the hours when it seems as if from out of nowhere the men and women of the night appear. Staggering across the stage to entertain the captured audience.

These strange, frightening figures are only just, but always, held together with bits of string. Grimly holding onto their life line, those mysterious bottles all wrapped up in newspaper. They all seem to spend their lives shadow boxing, spitting and slipping. Sometimes falling, crashing to the ground. All totally unreal to the uninitiated traveller.

Such a sight could only belong in a nightmare, these drunken misfits, life's refugees that nobody seems to want to help even if they could seem to surround us now. I wonder what you would do if presented with such a problem?

Coping with one of these strange beings can shatter the confidence of even the strongest amongst us. Their moods change from minute to minute, so what could you say that wouldn't send them into a fit of uncontrollable violence. I know this sounds a bit far fetched, but I have seen these sudden explosions of anger, so completely unpredictable and frightening. Panic stricken you decide it would be better after all if you keep moving, making sure that you never venture into that vulnerable position.

It was bad enough before, being stranded such a long way from home, I really didn't think things could get any worse . . . but I was wrong! By no stretch of the imagination could I foresee anything so sad and depressing. I seem to have lived my life with my head buried in the sand. From time to time I look up at the big clock, the hands of which seem to have completely stopped.

Hopelessly you start to feel the cold reality of the moment. Looking around I feel like a lost child, everyone has gone home but me . . . at least that's how it feels. All the small shops are empty now, the kind faces across the counter of the tea and coffee shop have long since gone . . . I wonder what they're doing now! I expect they're at home drinking tea and sitting by the fire . . . oh well.

Now it's down to survival of the fittest, instincts such as these used to be second nature, once upon a time. Somewhere along the line this particular animal called man decided to detach himself from the animal kingdom.

Looking around I watch this so-called civilised herd of wild animals starting to show their teeth. It's time to stand your ground against all the intruders, that's the order of the moment.

After a while the main bulk of the crowd were starting to separate into about three or four different categories. The most significant character in his heavenly overcast 'goon' show is the much travelled, cool, calm professional survivor.

This quiet gymnast of life takes each obstacle in his stride, never falters and always comes home victorious to collect his prize. 'First Prize' a place to sit out of the wet and cold, adequate provisions for a well ordered and not too uncomfortable night.

'Second Prize' and a close runner-up goes to the rough and tough, all-round bully, this ex-major or jumped up public school, chinless wonder. He tackles the same situation with the subtlety of a constipated orang-utan. Once stunning his prey with a velocity of decibels, the like not many of us mere mortals have ever experienced, he proceeds to brow beat and completely demoralise whoever tries to stop him getting his way. 'Second Prize' is achieved with the maximum of noise and bad taste. It has been said that this oral super man is nothing short of an all-round *rotter!*

The next two categories are not so much prizes as two very different classes of losers. So in 'Third' place we have the only real cop-out in this extravaganza in the survival game. This is the typical first class traveller, he is the amazing ever open cheque book, never rough it, top hat and tail merchant. I must say I am impressed by his total confidence, but I wonder how he would cope with the situation if, like most of us, he didn't have a never-ending supply of money to depend on. But I must admit he must be pretty resourceful to have made and kept his money in the first place. So a well earned 'Third' place goes to him.

'Fourth' place and all time loser goes to the master of complete confusion. This super flapper rushed from place to place like a demented fly, never stops complaining and always ends up at the bottom of the pile. I'm sure everybody has seen him, he's the bloke who always travels with about three or four suitcases all bursting at the seams. He has the same number of children running in different directions and all covered in chocolate, runny noses and orange squash. I can't help feeling sorry for this poor devil, because he never stood a chance in a situation like this. It's really an observation of life when you think about it, there are survivors, bullies, the rich and the poor. *No rules* just plain animal cunning.

This three ringed circus goes on non-stop all through the night. Mr 'First Prize' sits comfortably wrapped in confidence, smoking a cigarette, blowing smoke rings into the air looking very relaxed. Mr 'Second Prize' is sitting guarding his little patch of territory, glaring at anybody who dares to come within spitting distance. Mr 'Third Prize' I expect, is tucked up in a very nice bed at the Railway Hotel, completely oblivious to all the hardship and suffering of the poor old Mr 'Fourth Place'. By now the children have all nodded off, Fourth Place, himself, has tried a number of times in numerous positions, but he can't relax long enough to share the sheer luxury of that 'oh such sweet slumber' that his kids just tumble into, whenever the mood takes them.

Day breaks, pigeons have started to fly down from somewhere high up in the roof, swooping down like the first act in yet another stage extravaganza, I wonder what today will bring!

With searching eyes I look at the clock once more, it has just turned 5.30am, most people have been awake for hours but there are still a few with their eyes closed, mouths open, sleeping in fits and starts. The place is covered with empty coke tins, bits of cellophane, half chewed sandwiches and apple cores. It really does resemble a battle field. I look around and wonder how much longer it is going to be before we get our reprieve.

At 6 o'clock precisely the PA system suddenly comes alive. Excitement ripples through the vast dormitory of weary hopefuls. The announcer greets us all with an apologetic air, saying 'Good morning everybody, I trust you haven't spent the night too uncomfortably!'

There are a few half hearted word of reprisals, but by now everybody is just too tired to be bothered.

Taxis had started to arrive and so too had many tradesmen and the workers on the morning shift. Those who could afford a bit of breakfast queued up and quickly made off with their rich prizes of British Rail tea and broken biscuits. Down in the public conveniences people were trying to make themselves look, at least, as though they were in a fit condition to tackle the world.

There is always somebody in every crowd fully kitted out for any emergency, like the man with the electric razor, toothbrush (and paste) and a look of superiority to go with it. Others are making do, splashing their face with water and cleaning their teeth with a finger. It looked as though some people had spent all night down there. I can't say I would have relished the thought of that, but I can remember spending a night in a Lowestoft wash and brush up, but that wasn't too bad. I used old roller towels for warmth and as far as I can remember slept very well.

At 6.30 the PA crackled back into life again with the news we didn't think we would ever hear again, the work to rule was over and the trains were running as usual.

There was a sigh of relief and a surprising sound of exuberance and laughter. Straight away everybody started to sort themselves out, as if somebody had fired a starting pistol.

As usual the ones ready first were running to board their respective trains. Mr 'First Prize' was just getting settled in his carriage as Mr 'Second Prize' was still shouting the odds, something about the country going to the dogs. Mr 'Third Place' arrived by taxi, freshly groomed, paper under his arm, not a hair out of place. Mr 'Fourth Place', well you can imagine! There was shouting, crying, pushing and shoving with cries of 'Why me?' as if he was the only one.

It's gone 7.30 now and everybody has successfully scrambled aboard their respective trains and are clattering towards their homes. I'm sure some of them must have thought at least once that night that they would never see their homes again.

Home now, sitting by a large and friendly fire, thinking, I wonder how all those other stories ended up. Happy I hope, but I doubt it!

B109

David Daniels

It stood there in the park, vanish fading, bronze plate framed in bright green, every day it received whatever English weather was in store. The tarmacamed path formed a thoroughfare where it made an appreciated sojourn, sometimes ignored, sometimes used.

Two young people, both in their twenties, smartly dressed in office garb, approach the bench from opposite directions, both heads down, one in a book, one in a newspaper. They sit down almost simultaneously, one at each end of B109.

The girl, pretty with a thin nose and angular face, looks up and then turns slowly, starting slightly.

'Jason, what are you doing?' She stares, wide-eyed.
'Reading my paper at lunchtime, you?'
'Here, I mean,' the girl frowns.
'I work here - often come here to read, relax; dilutes the nonsense of the morning.' The young man, Crombie clad, looks at the girl with bored eyes; young, short black hair and a long intelligent face.
'So, dear Rachel, *fancy that!'* He smirks at her still staring face.
'I don't actually, once in a decade would be too often,' a slight scowl spoils her neat features.
'How's romance?' Jason feels pleased.
'None of your business, how's shallowness and lack of commitment?' she smiles briefly.
'Still shallow, not committed,' he says, voice monotone, 'so who is he and does he know?'
'Know what? How lucky he is?'
'No, what he's in for.'
'Go to hell!'
'Not yet, not until I've lived a little. No, really, I'd like to know.'

She smirks, thinking of him, 'He's got his own car leasing business, wealthy, a real man, knows how to treat a girl, make her feel wanted.'
'Sounds a bore,' Jason says, thinking of the two of them when they were together. 'Not as good as us though,' he says, hoping.

'We were never good: necessity in the remotest way described us; a page of my life, coffee-stained, uninteresting, ignored, instantly forgotten. You're mentioned many times in it.'
'Aww,' he says, sticking out his lower lip, 'first love usually is cumbersome, you know.'
'You like to flatter yourself, don't you? If I had been I'd have been seriously damaged; as it was I hardly noticed you passing,' she says, sniffing.
'Like to go for a drink some time, just for ol-' he raises one eyebrow, mouth open in mid-sentence.
'No I wouldn't,' she shouts, making a group of schoolgirls sitting on the grass behind them turn around, then look at each other and giggle. She rises and starts to walk away.
'Guess I'll have to burn the love letters,' he says, smirking.

It's some time hence: a cold winter's morning and the bench is covered with a crystalline whiteness, bearing a resemblance to granulated quartz. When the sunlight hits it, every colour in the visible spectrum is reflected off. To one side, the right, lies a small soft case, black, with a handle and shoulder strap. Embossed on the lower front is the name of a well-known computer manufacturer.

A tall, lanky youth, baseball cap reversed on his head, baggy clothes billowing, reversed-sail effect, rollerblades toward the bench and sees the case. Stopping, he looks around and then expertly brakes, landing lightly with a twist on the bench. He gingerly opens the case, head ducked down; an observer would think there were low-flying aircraft around. He slides a notebook computer out of the case, plastic meeting nylon causes a swishing. He clicks open the computer, then realises where he is and slots the computer back home. Rising with the help of braking wheels, he humps the case over his shoulder, knowing about fragility and glides off smoothly. The setting sun creates a golden aura round the silhouette.

The next day a middle-aged gentleman, cashmere overcoat collared with a scarlet, high quality scarf, walks with a disciplined walk to B109. He sits down with a thump, frowning, hands wrung slowly as he twists his wrist and sees the time. Ten minutes pass, then he yawns but still looks straight ahead. A small boy, no more than ten but not looking it in height, skips along the path and, seeming to ignore the gentleman, sits down alongside.

'Hi, you the guy my friend called?' says the boy with a childish, vulnerable voice, deep south Yankee accented.
'I am,' the man says looking around, taken aback, 'you are the contact?' Eyebrows are raised and the hand-wringing stops.
'This is a sample of what we have,' the boys says, handing over an A4 envelope.

The man opens the envelope and slides out a copy of a document, with a colour picture of a missile in the middle of the text. He reads the content briefly, looks at the picture, flushes and looks around again.

'You friend isn't a patriot, then?' he tries, smiling briefly and thinly.
'Do me a favour,' the boy says smirking, 'and don't try to get at him through me: I'm not a citizen or a resident of this naff-climated little island. We want one hundred grand now and the same on delivery, our choice of drop.' He looks at the man hard, body tensed and face serious.

The man scoffs, 'I don't have any money with me, we don't do that sort of thing.' He opens his hands as he talks.
'Then *you'd* better *start.* Tomorrow, drop the money in Lansing Street car park skip, 2.00pm. *We* sniff a fiddle and you'll read about it in Gadaffi's favourite rag.' The boy gets up and walks away, ignoring the man, now open-mouthed.

The man gets up, head hung down and walks off, sighing.

Some point in the future: a middle-aged woman walks to the bench and sits down. She fidgets, looks ahead and seems far away; she opens her handbag and takes out a smart mobile phone, one of the miniaturised flip variety and dials a number, fingers skipping expertly over the minute buttons. The ringing tone could be heard by anyone standing nearby but the few people that do pass are uninterested.
'Hello, Julie. Sharon. Listen, are you busy, can you lend me an ear or -'
Mumbling at the other end, then a few clear words.
'Great.'
A few words - tones of comfort are apparent.
'No, really, I'm fine. Look, you know how I've been whinging about work. Well -'

More words, some stated in surprise.
'No, I've not done anything yet but that awful new supervisor . . . ' (interruptions), 'yes, that's her, well, she's really becoming an unbearable pain. I went to the boss yesterday to discuss her and got no joy at all; I found out after from Alison that they're bosom buddies: who said cronyism was dead, eh?'

Some more words, concern clear.
'Yes, well, I hear you but, well, bullying at work exists, we all know it does. She likes me giving her my reports so she can hand them to our leader. I'm sure she just does it to take the credit. This morning she gave me a dressing down for being two minutes late; couldn't get a word in. I've tried talking to her but she just cuts me dead; it's the end, I've had enough.'

A few words of resignation.
'Quitter? No! I've tried everything. I know she wins but, well, most of the staff seem to hate her so I'm hardly a force of one am I?'
A few questioning words.
'Oh, I know what I'm going to do, resign and go to college: do something I like and enjoy.'
Another question.
'I have thought it through: best and most important decision in my life. Hey, how are you for a drink tonight?'
A moment's hesitation, then a few words.
'Okay, I'll see you at our wine bar at eight. Don't be late.'
The girl rings off, then sits for a moment, seemingly deep in thought. She stands, half smiling, half frowning, puts the phone away and strides off.

Later that afternoon, two workmen potter along the path, look at the bench from a distance and then approach, sitting down.
'What do you think, Sid?' says the taller of the two, a pot belly just starting to overhang the wide leather belt around his waist.
'What does the planner say?' His colleague, Sid, is thinner, black hair going grey but eyes retaining every bit of brightness and sharpness.
'Oh, he wants it over there,' Stan says pointing.
'In the middle of the park? There's no path anywhere near, and you know the complaints we get about dog mess.'

Stan opens his palms, resignedly: 'I know, I've told him and just about anyone else who will listen: the bench gets a lot of use, particularly at lunch time and weekends. Sometimes their logic seems so stupid.'

'Every time I walk along here, I see two people sitting having a deep-meaning conversation. It's a pleasure to think we make it possible for them to do that.'

'What would you like to do?' Stan has no ideas of his own but is willing to listen; he looks at his mate, curious.

'Well, you know that new outside theatre, they're going to build over there?' Sid says quietly, looking around.

'The Castleton Open Air, you mean? I thought that plan had been shelved.'

'Not according to my son Nigel. He's to be a member of the company and they say they have all the backing they need. All that is left is the necessary technical, financial and planning support and to start building.'

'So what's your idea?'

'To leave the bench where it is and build the theatre around it. Sure, the seats need raising but that would be a cakewalk for the American civil contractors involved. I've written to the mayor and he's investigating.'

'In the meantime we move it?'

'No we don't. We save the taxpayer and the post office a huge investment in time and effort and *leave* it.'

'Post office?'

'It's the most popular drop-off point in the town.'

'And the planner will agree?'

'He will if he doesn't want to be Castleton's first face-to-face agony aunt,' Sid says, getting up and following his mate along the path.

Greedy Gail
Vance A Carson

Gail McConachy, 'Greedy Gail' as she was known at school, had always been a glutton, be it an overeater of food or an overindulger in sensory pleasure. At Cardonald Comprehensive Gail was known to both the canteen staff and lusty boys alike. Dinner ladies would dish her out extra potions of custard and sponge, before Gail herself would become a giggling dessert behind the bike sheds. An activity which didn't earn Gail many friends. Too much cake and too much kissing never produces too much friendship. At least not in the playground.

As a teenager the somewhat large Miss McConachy had left school with no qualifications and little prospect of future employment. Being heart lazy was second nature to Greedy Gail, whilst eating as much as possible remained her primary ambition. The boys had dropped away now. Gail had become more than easy, much more, possibly 9 stones more than any other girl the same age. Gail had become an obese obscenity. A person interested in her own selfish desires and wanton gluttony. Most alarmingly though, Gail had become obsessed with food and gambling. The food provided an inner feeling of warmth and satisfaction, whilst gambling provided an outlet for her previously carnal lust. Screaming at a horse being whipped around a two mile race course was more than enough physical stimulation for someone who regarded going to the toilet as an aerobic exercise.

Using her elderly mother's purse to finance her weekly trips to the bookmakers, Gail was committed to gambling in every form. She'd put a £20 bet on the morning handicap, spent three hours at the bingo hall and relax in a greasy chip shop for the rest of the day. There she'd sit surrounded by egg, chips, sausage and beans, and various magazines offering cash prizes for the completion of crosswords and puzzles. And so became Gail's usual routine. Scratch cards and sausages, horses and hamburgers. All fuelled by her dear old mother's disability allowance. An allowance both Mrs McConachy and Miss McConachy claimed was necessary, as they were both far too fat to work. Yet although she had never followed the avenue of paid employment, life was hard for Greedy Gail, finding a taxi to take her home from the bookies could take at least half an hour some days.

In her adult years Gail was increasingly haunted by the guilt surrounding her mother's death, and the thought that she may have abused the old woman's generosity at times. Greedy Gail had also grown to gargantuan proportions and hardly ever left the comfort of her sweaty living room. Her solitude and slumber had produced a life of self loathing where exercise and even washing had become an unthinkable chore. And yet the gambling remained. To win a fortune on the lottery was now her only hope of salvation. It was the only option for a woman who had become a hermit on debt mountain, and who desperately needed major liposuction just to ensure a few more years of life without saturated fat in her arteries and veins.

Being the kind of person who would be described as insecure and gullible by every known advertising corporation on earth, Gina was also to become rather interested in the occult and the magical powers of fortune telling. A carefully worded advertisement in one of her usual puzzle magazines even promised to change her life for the price of a long distance call. An offer Gail found hard to resist, being that she could resist nothing except self control. Madam Zola's colourful advert also informed Gail that all major credit cards would be accepted. So the phone call was made and credit card details exchanged. After four of five minutes of creepy music, piped down the phone at Gail's expense, the great and mysterious Madam Zola was engaged in the twentieth reading of the day.

'Don't worry me dear, your future is all here in front of me and it's looking rosy,' said she, spreading her tarot cards into the shape of a Celtic Cross.
'Oh Madam Zola,' Gail began to sob, 'I hope you're right, my life is so miserable.'
'Trust in the tarot,' replied the woman on the other end of the phone, who was also struggling to maintain a shaky Romanian accent. 'You're in luck, I see the Queen of Cups before me, money will shortly follow my dear.'

Gail listened intently to the fortune teller's speech about Princes and Swords and Chariots and Wands, before the mention of one card in particular raised questions in Gail's head.

'What did you say the last card was Madam Zola? Something about a skeleton?'
'Yes me dear, that's the Death card, but nothing to be worried about. Death simply means the end of your old ways and the beginning of the new. Out goes your sadness, in comes the gladness.'

Madam Zola's phone indicated that there was yet another gullible punter waiting for her life to change on line two.

'Well me dear,' said the clairvoyant in a now obviously Glaswegian accent, 'that's all the tarot will foretell today, so take care of yourself and look forward to your coming wealth, blessed be.'
'Blessed be,' Gail replied in respect to the Wiccan tradition she'd often read about.

The phone call to the fortune teller was a source of internal dispute for several weeks. Gail just could not decide whether or not to believe Zola's prediction, being that it was probably just too good to be true. She recalled a TV programme about magic which she'd watched when her mother was still alive. Apparently fairground or telephone fortune tellers are highly likely to say exactly what their customers want to hear. Being that a prediction of someone's impending doom would not be good for future business in the fortune telling trade. After all, no one truly wants to be told of the future misery which they can do nothing about anyway. However, the TV programme did suggest that a fortune teller who tells of an exact event on a precise date will probably be telling the truth. The less vague a prediction the more easy it is to call a fortune teller a fraud if the event or action in question never unfolds. Therefore, if a fortune teller says someone will eat steak on their next birthday, chances are that they are a con merchant using the image of clairvoyance to make money from emotionally turbulent souls. However, if a fortune teller tells a client that they *will be a steak* on their next birthday, the client would be strongly advised to stay away from starving cannibals.

Madam Zola's prediction had been vague, very vague, and yet Gail would not give up the belief that her fortune was to change for the better. Using her dwindling credit resources and disability income, Gail spent weeks filling in even more puzzles and crossword competitions. She bet on at least three horses a day, making good use of the internet gambling sites she had found on her keyboard worn computer. Gail had also bought more scratch cards and lottery tickets in the weeks following the phone call to Madam Zola than she had done in the previous six months. Even Merlin's eldritch wand could not have brought a more speedy profit to Camelot than Madam Zola's phone.

With debt and bills piling higher than ever before, Gail was becoming increasingly depressed. It had been three months since she was informed of her change of fortune and of her rosy wealth to come, and yet all she had witnessed was the gloom of financial misery and a further increase of weight on her hips. The balance of desire between lottery tickets and ready meals was beginning to tip to the side of spending all her money on microwavable food, and completely forget the lottery dream.

Gail would give the lottery option just one more chance however. The chosen date of her monetary juggle with the lotto's magically numbered balls was obvious, at least to someone with an interest in the occult. October 31st Hallowe'en, and the amazing mid-week guaranteed millions.

The preparation for Hallowe'en was soon complete and everything was set for the big night in. Gail had spent her whole disability allowance on forty lottery tickets, seven giant bags of chilli flavoured tortilla chips and spicy dip for each, four two litre bottles of Coke, two Indian curries and a bottle of Asda champagne. A treat waiting on ice to celebrate the dawn of her new life, when the moment came for the six numbers of glory to be named on live television. Getting into the spirit of the occasion she had even purchased three giant pumpkins from the supermarket's home delivery service. Never making any claims to be an artist didn't stop her from carving smiling faces on the orange coloured fruit, as she scooped out the pulp from within. She was momentarily pleased at her flickering candle-lit lanterns as she sipped a mug of freshly boiled pumpkin soup.

Tonight my new life begins, she thought.

Three more hours of eating passed until the time of the big draw came. Gail turned up the volume on her TV set, placed herself in the middle of the buckled sofa surrounded by crisps and tortilla chips, fanned out her lottery tickets in both of her chubby little hands, and waited to be rich.

'Happy Hallowe'en everybody,' gleamed an ageing celebrity chef as he introduced the night's entertainment at lottery headquarters.

It seemed ironic that a chef would be the one to make Greedy Gail's dreams come true, being that she had been encouraged to eat her way to obesity by watching the carnival of culinary delights conjured up by smiling groups of celebrity chefs over the past ten to fifteen years.

'He's better at cooking than presenting,' Gail muttered to herself as she opened up a new packet of crisps.

After several cloned plastic dance acts had mimed their way through a musical pop routine, the moment came at last for the lottery balls to be drawn. At last this was the moment Greedy Gail had waited for. At last this was the moment Miss McConachy had nurtured in her dreams. Dreams where she was as thin as the girl next door. At last this was the moment that was predicted by Madam Zola and her esoteric spread of tarot cards. The new dawn awaited.

'Tonight's numbers are 5, 23, 34, 3, 12, 33 and the bonus number 17, in ascending order that's . . . '

It didn't matter what the ascending order was. Gail soon switched off the television because it was all over anyway. She had picked the birthdays of her favourite celebrities to give her the lottery numbers displayed on the forty tickets in front of her. None of the birthdays matched the complete set of drawn numbers. She had not won a fortune. She had not won anything. Fate had mocked her yet again. Madam Zola had obviously told her a pack of lies. The Celtic Cross spread had been false, as had Gail's hopes for the future. Her sinful life of greed was to continue on a budget of debt and poverty. It was not a happy Hallowe'en.

Slouched in a blanket of tortilla crumbs and half-eaten biscuits Gail continued to munch on a handful of smoky bacon crisps. It was all she could do to compose herself in the company of three Hallowe'en lanterns which seemed to laugh at her misfortune from the corner of the room. Eating and overeating had been a way of life for Gail for as long as she could remember, and now it looked as if there was to be no escape from her daily cupboard and fridge odyssey of greed.

As she munched into yet more handfuls of crisps Gail suddenly found that she could no longer breath. Something was lodged firmly in her throat and no amount of coughing was helping matters. About two or three minutes of extreme distress followed as Gail McConachy tried to steal a breath free from the crumbling snack food which she'd stuffed into her mouth only moments before. It occurred that the last mental image Gail would focus on before her subsequent demise would be the skeleton card of death, as predicted by a fortune teller's tarot deck.

At her autopsy, the district coroner explained that Miss McConaughy's death had been caused by a tiny plastic envelope which had become lodged in her trachea. The lethal envelope contained a neatly folded cheque for two million pounds sterling, which was the grand prize in a crisp company's advertising promotion. Sadly this cheque had been swallowed in Gail's haste to feed both her greed and sadness.

Madam Zola still operates her telephone fortune telling service, and is rumoured to appear on a future episode of the National Lottery's live prize draw, as a guest clairvoyant.

Just Another Tourist

Don Woods

James Tillis pulled onto the garage forecourt attached to the motel and topped his camper up with petrol before driving on to the parking area provided for those who wished to sleep overnight. It had been a long drive down from North Sweden where he had been taking his annual three weeks holiday, tomorrow he would reach the ferry to take him across the North sea and back to England. He decided to have a drink in the motel as he was not going to be driving that night. Finding himself a seat by the window so that he could observe the camper, he ordered a beer.

It was an hour and four beers later, he noticed the grey Mercedes pull up behind his camper. For about ten minutes it stood there, then two men and a girl got out, and he had the distinct impression they were studying the camper with more than the normal amount of curiosity that a tourist's camper would invoke. They entered the restaurant and chose a table alongside his own facing the parking area, which struck him as odd as the place was practically empty. One of the men caught his eye and smiled, raising his glass as he did so, 'You are English?' he asked, 'Is that your camper out there?'

'Yes! I am English, is it that obvious,' James replied.

The stranger laughed. 'No, we saw the GB sticker on the back, and were admiring the many other stickers you have, you certainly have travelled to a lot of places in our country.'

'Yes, that is the beauty of owning a camper, it gives you the freedom to travel about, but I am at the end of my holiday now, tomorrow I catch the ferry back to England.'

The stranger gave a look to his two companions that James felt was more than just a casual glance, then he said, 'I notice you are drinking, so I guess you will be staying the night here then knowing the strict rules on drink driving here in Sweden, so why don't you come and join us, as we are staying the night too, we have rooms booked.'

'I would love to,' replied James picking up his beer and joining them.

Their names were Lars, Tom and Marit, and they had been on a business course. They were charming company and the night flew by. Lars insisted that James try some of their local moonshine that Marit

was carrying in her bag. James had heard of this stuff and how potent it was supposed to be, but had never tried it. He was soon quite drunk and made his apologies to them. 'I have had far too much to drink so I will say good night, as I have an early start in the morning.'
They insisted he had one more shot of the moonshine before he left and as he drank, and drunk as he was, James knew they had given him an extra large one, and sensed they were trying to get him drunk, and he didn't think it was out of friendship!
'Come on,' Marit said laughing, 'I will walk you back across the car park, while the boys organise our rooms.'
Fumbling with his key James finally got the door open and collapsed on the bed, Marit threw a cover over him and left to join the others.

Back at the restaurant she said, 'He is out like a light, let's get the stuff fixed and move away from here.'

If James could have seen what happened next he would have been amazed as they opened the boot of the Mercedes and removed several packages, these Lars and Tom proceeded to secrete underneath the camper. Once that was done they climbed into their car and disappeared into the night.

In the morning James woke with a shocking headache, there was no sign of the Mercedes. As he sat having a coffee he thought of the previous night, he was convinced they had got him drunk on purpose, but why? And why the interest in the camper, a feeling of unease went through him as he thought of a possible reason, he went outside and peered under the camper, at first seeing nothing then he caught a glimpse of white plastic above the petrol tank. He wiggled underneath and removed a packet, it was drugs, he had seen enough in his time to recognise it, there were several more packets. He replaced the packet and thought what to do next. What if they would be watching him from the ferry port?

Taking a piece of paper he wrote a note, this he put in his passport. Then set off. It was very rare he got stopped by the customs, so as he approached their office he dived from the cab and stuck his open passport with the note held firmly by his thumb, through the open window where the officer sat. The startled officer was about to say it did not need stamping when he saw the note in which James had explained about the drugs. He discreetly removed the note and made a big show of stamping his passport, then asked him to continue his journey as normal.

Driving off the ferry in England, James saw the Mercedes pull out after him, and at a discreet distance follow him until he reached his home, then they disappeared.

It was three in the morning when he heard the shouts and slamming of car doors as the British customs officers caught the three in the act of removing the drugs. And as they were led struggling away he said to them, 'Thanks for the drinks, it is not often people will buy a customs officer drinks, even if he is on holiday.'
And as if to rub salt in the wounds the officer in charge saluted him and said 'See you at work on Monday Sir.'

THE WOUNDED
Mike Smith

Oryctolagus Cuniculus of the family *Leporidae.*
A somewhat grand title for a very common little beastie that roams the Highlands of Scotland, the Rabbit. The rabbit, so we are led to believe, is a very simple, uncomplicated creature. He eats almost non-stop. He breeds almost non-stop. Farmers loathe them, but children adore them. They appear to be reasonably intelligent when it comes to avoiding natural enemies such as the scavenging crow or the beady-eyed hawk, but the rabbit fails miserably when he happens upon one of mankind's great inventions, the car, and that's where our story begins.

It was a clear, crispy cold night when Joshua left. The children were being their noisy, boisterous selves as he said goodbye to his mate Rooah at the entrance of the burrow. Above the playful screams of the children, Rooah had issued her usual stern warning to Joshua about the dangers of travelling at night, and especially of crossing the hard earth that humans drove their machines on.

Joshua gave her a reassuring nod, then quickly made his way up the hill. When he reached the top, he turned and looked down. Rooah, as ever, was still there watching, waiting for him to disappear from sight. He hated to go, but what else could he do?

The humans in the nearby town were building at such a rate, that it was only a matter of time until they came upon the burrow and destroyed it. Not intentionally, for man has never been a real enemy of the rabbit, but man builds and expands without thinking of the consequences for the natural world, and its order. Joshua had put this moment off for a long time, but new earth for a burrow had to be found, and found quickly.

The moon had grown darker and had all but disappeared by the time Joshua had found what he had been looking for. 'Perfect,' he whispered to himself as he gazed at the bracken-covered hillside.

A small stream that danced merrily down the opposite side of the hill would provide them with all the water they would need. Age-old gorse bushes, with strong, deep roots, meant there would be strength in the earth below for the main burrow and its various antechambers. Joshua took one last look, then turned to start the long journey home.

Cold, biting rain now soaked into Joshua's fur as he scampered over the rock-strewn glen. Every so often he would stop, shake the ice-cold rain from his coat, and listen. For though it was dark and late at night, his enemies never slept. In the distance, he could see light that moved, which meant he was near to the hard, grey earth that humans travelled on. But it also meant he was nearer to home, and perhaps it was the thought of home, and the love and warmth that awaited him, that distracted Joshua for a split-second.

It only took a moment, but in that fragment of time, lives were about to be changed . . . forever.

The human didn't stop. After all, he was in a hurry, and it was only a rabbit.

Joshua lay paralysed. The dampness from the hard grey earth seeped into every part of his broken body, making him quiver. 'Must try and move,' he thought, but it was useless. A last hope was to call Rooah, and perhaps the night wind would carry his cry to the burrow, but try as he might, no sound came from him. 'It is finished,' he thought. 'Soon other humans will come. Some will see me and avoid me, but others . . . they will say, it's only a rabbit.'

Joshua's thoughts now turned to other dangers. His enemies, the crow and the hawk. Soon they would gather and circle overhead. Soon the feast would begin.

From somewhere in the darkness, Joshua detected a sound. Softly at first, like a gentle breeze singing through the branches of a tree, but then louder and louder like an angry wind. 'My enemies come,' he thought. Unable to move, Joshua waited for them to strike, but instead of a razor-like claw tearing into his lifeless body, he felt himself moving. Slowly at first, but then with a sense of urgency. Then he heard her voice.
'Joshua please try and move,' it was Rooah. Somehow, during the night, she had sensed something was wrong and had set off to meet him. Using her nose, Rooah continued to push.
'We have to get off the hard earth, come on Joshua, try!' she pleaded, but it was no use.

Suddenly, she stopped. Her large brown ears had picked up a sound, a familiar sound. Joshua heard it too. It was a car.

Rooah pushed frantically. Her claws were splitting and tearing off on the hard surface of the road. The lights from the approaching car bounced off the surrounding hillside, getting closer with every frantic breath she took. Joshua wanted to scream, 'Leave me, save yourself!' but it was too late, the headlights of the car had reached them.

Joshua could hear Rooah groan with agony as she pushed and pushed in a last effort to reach safety. Then suddenly, the car slowed down, and stopped. Joshua could just make out the image of the human in the car. Both of his hands were grasping the steering wheel, as though he were afraid to let go. Rooah started to push again, just a few more feet and they would be safe.

Two yellow lights blinked off and on in the darkness. Rooah wondered what they were, but kept on pushing.

She stopped when a light from the interior of the car illuminated the human, and for the first time, she could see his face.

The road system in Argyll is known throughout the civilised world as having three major defects, and they are, potholes, narrow carriageways, and local drivers, who think they know everything! John Cummings fell into the latter category.

It was a miserable night, which perfectly complimented the miserable day John Cummings had just experienced.

Hell, he shouldn't even be on the road. He should be tucked up in bed in the Argyll Arms Hotel. A whisky and soda in one hand, and a signed contract from Barclay engineering in the other. But no, the job had been lost to a firm of suppliers from the south of England, and all for the sake of a few hundred pounds!

Every time he thought of it, poison flowed into his veins. He had spent weeks working on the quotation. Carefully checking and rechecking his figures, taking a bit off here, and adding a bit on there, until he thought it was unbeatable.

Hours were spent buttering up old Barclay, taking him and that pretentious wife of his out to lunches and dinners, only to discover the old goat was getting the same treatment from a firm of outsiders!

How the hell was he going to explain it to his bosses?

He could just imagine what Dunsford, his area manager would say, or more to the point, what he wouldn't say.

'God, I'm going to look like a complete bloody amateur!' he thought. And of course, there was Patricia, his wife. She already had the bonus off this contract well and truly spent!

'Oh Lord, she's going to have a fit!' he sighed, slowing down for yet another pothole. 'Bloody roads! Bloody Barclays!' he screamed. 'Gotta calm down, gotta think this through,' he said aloud.

John lit up a cigarette and switched the radio on. What he needed was some nice, calming background music to soothe his weary soul, but all he got was some smarmy sounding, late night DJ, prattling on about how life was so good. 'Yeah right!' he snarled, switching the radio off.

Outside the car, the weather took a turn for the worse. Heavy, driving rain battered against the windshield.

'Terrific,' he mumbled, 'the end of a perfect day. No contract, no bonus, no bloody luck!'

After a while, the dark imaginations of a tired mind began to surface. What if head office sacked him because of this? Where would he find another job? God, the mortgage! How could he pay it, and Patricia, bloody hell! She couldn't cope with a husband on the dole or being forced to live in some crappy council house. After seven years of marriage he knew her well enough to know she couldn't handle a life of reduced circumstances. Rats and sinking ships sprung to mind. 'A sinking ship, yeah, that just about sums it up,' he thought.

A feeling of complete and utter despair now occupied every corner of John's mind. Now the dream of a glittering career, of being a good provider, of having achieved something to be proud of, had disappeared, only to be replaced with a sense of hopelessness, worthlessness and fear.

As the car twisted and turned on the narrow road, John could see glimpses of light in the distance, not far to go now. He glanced at the clock on the dashboard. 1.30am. 'God, if only I could turn back time I could . . . ' but he never finished his thought. His eyes had spotted something lying in the road. He slowed down. There was something else there, something moving. 'What is that?' he whispered. John slowed down to a crawl, then stopped.

'What the hell?' he exclaimed. Two rabbits were in the middle of the road. One rabbit was using its nose to push an injured rabbit off the road. John hauled himself closer to the windscreen, hardly believing the drama that was unfolding. 'It's trying to get it off the road!' he cried. 'Bloody hell!'

Aware that other cars may be around, even at this late hour, John switched on his hazard warning lights and continued to watch. The smaller of the two rabbits that was doing the pushing was having a hard time moving, what John could only presume, was its mate. He could see its paws slipping on the wet surface of the road as it pushed and nudged the other rabbit towards the edge of the road. A strange, overwhelming urge to do something, anything, swept over John, but what?

Gingerly, he opened his door. Just a crack, but enough for the interior light to come on. The rabbit stopped pushing, turned towards the car and stared at John. And on that wet and windswept Highland road, in a magical moment of time, a man saw the light through the eyes of a frightened animal, and the animal saw the spirit of man at his very best.

Slowly, John moved towards the rabbits. All thoughts of Barclays and lost contracts and bonuses had disappeared. He knew what he had to do; he knew what he wanted to do.

As he approached them, the rabbit that had been pushing bolted to the side of the road and stopped. John bent down and gently picked up the injured rabbit. He could feel it trembling as he held it in his arms. He walked carefully to where its mate was waiting and placed it gently on the grass. John gave the injured rabbit a gentle stroke. No words were spoken, for none were necessary, but in his heart, he wished it well.

The Simple Code

D Brain

Whether Robert suffered a bout of insanity or his temper let rip is an open question, the result was twofold, an officer with a sore nose and a colourful eye. The Court Marshall which followed for reasons best known to himself granted him parole and before it was reconveyed Robert had been discharged from the RAF.

Over the previous six months I had encountered Robert on a number of occasions as a second class general duty airman he stoked the combustion stoves, emptied the waste paper baskets and after a fashion swept the floor of the Nissen Hut which served as an office.

His happy smile, dancing blue eyes fascinated me, when he spoke he was polite without being serville. One morning he came close enough to my desk to slip a bar of milk chocolate under a pile of files, stepping back, he placed a finger on his lips whispering, 'The wrapping says it all.'

At the monthly Officers' Mess Dance he served as the cloakroom attendant, soon after the incident of the chocolate, one dance evening was remarkable in that one of the girls - Thelma, tore her dress. I accompanied her to the cloakroom. Robert saw Thelma's tear and being told why he literally pushed her into a chair, his single word 'Sit' sounding like an order to a dog.

A minute later he was on his knees, the torn pieces in his hand. For five minutes I watched in amazement as deftly using a needle, he made a respectable repair. 'There you are Madam,' he said as he stood up. 'A blind man would be pleased to see it.'

Thelma stood up, shook herself and walked off without a word of thanks, leaving me to gasp and ask, 'Where did you learn to do that?'
'At my mother's knee - this repair kit went everywhere with us. 'Never know' she used to say 'when one of you lot will need it.'

His slow, soft voice and momentary watery eye struck a cord of sympathy, I would have liked to have continued the conversation but others wanted his attention.

Our next meeting had been in the office when again he stopped in front of me, 'I've come to say thank you - I am being kicked out tomorrow.' As he spoke, once again, he slipped a bar of chocolate onto my desk and continued. 'It's the wrapping not the contents which count.'

I fingered the chocolate bar for some seconds before I slipped it into my handbag. Later I would study it closely.

I did my best to forget Robert. We were socially opposites, there was little about his appearance to commend him to anyone - especially my parents. Neither do officers 'keep company with other ranks'. I knew nothing about his medical discharge. When he repaired Thelma's dress, his actions had been swift - deliberate and assured in his ability. As for the chocolates I tried to convince myself he meant nothing more than a friendly act.

I dithered six weeks and wrote to him via RAF records, writing relieved an inner tension, waiting for a reply created another. When it came it was in two parts in separate envelopes. The first merely said 'Take care of chocolates, Robert'. The other was equally brief. 'CO giving you leave, arrive Canal Wharf before 4pm. McMavis leaves prompt.' The CO refused to enlighten me.

McMavis proved to be a 70ft canal barge 2/3rds open to the elements. Aft of this a small cabin, the engine covering and an open cockpit large enough for two, one whom could operate the tiller.

A dozen of us crowded into that cabin. When Robert appeared he ignored us all, unhitched the ropes, started the motor and stood in the cockpit, eyes fixed ahead.

Of that journey I remember little, the smell of an oily engine, mixed with that of a smelly gentleman who had had one over the eight. The noise came not from the engine, but the rain, the roar of thunder and the fear of lightning.

When we stopped there was a hasty exit of passengers but it was not until the last had gone that Robert grabbed my arm. 'Come on lass - a two minute dash and you can dry off.'

Once in the kitchen of what he called his 'bachelor pad' he left me to fiddle with the Rayburn fire, while he fetched some things from another room. Upon opening the door to another he shouted, 'Plenty of hot water, hot towel on the rail and a dressing gown behind the door. Help yourself.'

Not only was I drenched to the skin, I was terrified what sort of a maniac was Robert. I had a headache. He had given me no word of greeting and he left me with what sounded like an order. I was still standing like a statue when he returned with my two suitcases. I was still in the same position when he returned the second time. I wanted to scream but his stinging words and acts stirred me into action.

'Look lass - there's the bathroom, at least put a comb through your hair, I am stripping off here.'

As he spoke he flung his sodden jacket over the back of a chair, he stooped to take off his heavy boots and it was as he slipped his braces off his shoulders that I beat a hasty retreat.

I enjoyed that bath when I timidly joined him. I should have laughed. I was wearing his heavy blanket dressing gown with little else underneath. He was in his pyjamas, a knee length butcher's apron tied round his waist, his gorgeous slippers were more suited to my bare feet. I also enjoyed the feast he had prepared.

Sitting back in his chair he declared, 'I was ready for that.'
'Bang goes your rations for a month,' I tried to smile as he chuckled.
'The chicken will have laid another batch of eggs by tomorrow,' as he continued he stroked his chin with his left hand. 'Tomorrow I leave here at 7pm. Back by nine. in the afternoon I leave here at 2.30, back the same as today, care to come for the ride?'
He must have seen me shudder.
'You missed the scenery, the canal breezes and nobody was in the mood for talking - it was one hell of a voyage.'

I made the effort to clear the table and he joined me at the sink. 'Jennifer,' he said, using my Christian name for the first time, 'this week may be a difficult one for us both, but I promise to treat you as a sister in word and deed.' He sighed a deep long sigh before adding, 'I asked the powers that be for your company, thanks for coming.'

'Does Thelma come into this - she was on the train.'

Nothing marred our six days together. I enjoyed the daily boat trips, made friends with the passengers. Only once did Robert leave me to wander around on my own, even then I was befriended.

Two days into my return to duty I was called into the CO's office. With him was one of the gentlemen who had been a regular passenger, his wife keeping me company when Robert was away.

'Mr Jackson,' I heard the CO say, 'has given you an excellent reference and I agree you should be offered promotion. But,' he paused to glance at Mr Jackson. 'The day you left Robert, the barge was blown up.'

I wobbled, I gasped, I stuttered. 'Is he safe?'
'Yes, we had a minute to disembark everybody.'
'Was it Thelma?'
'And her boyfriend - they were after you.'
'Me - why me?'
'Matter of a torn dress. We let it be known that you had removed a slim film tucked into the hem. In fact Robert did and handed it over to us. Robert was concerned for your safety. Did you read the messages on the chocolate wrappings?'
'Was the Court Marshall and medical discharge part of his cover story?'
'Amateur Dramatics are his passion.'
'Why?' I continued to question only vaguely aware of what was being said. 'Why pick on me as a stooge?'
'You were Thelma's friend, when the film went missing we let it be known you had it, in fact, Robert passed it to us. When you run off to Robert, she followed. She lost you in the storm, we also lost her. Friday, she and her boyfriend hitched a lift on the barge and were arrested just as the boat sailed. It was too late to do anything about the fireworks,' the CO paused, glanced at his companion and smiled a broad, wide smile. 'Now we have a greater problem, do you want to be posted near to Robert or a long way away?'

THE ELEVENTH STATION

Nicola Grant

It was a cold, damp and drizzly morning. Harry and Andrew had been planning to go moor walking. They would probably have put it off and waited for more auspicious weather had it not been the last day of their holiday. Tomorrow their cases and trunks would be packed and they would be boarding a steam train heading south. They both felt that it would be a pity to waste the last day of their holiday indoors, playing cards and drinking cocoa. Perhaps the weather would clear and if it worsened, they could accept defeat and return to their lodgings.

The two men headed off determined to make the most of their last day in the glorious, if somewhat rain-soaked, English countryside. They walked out of the village and down winding, twisting country lanes. They had planned a circuitous route which would lead them around a large area of moorland and then back to the village; hopefully they would be back in time for tea and a nice hotpot or casserole would be waiting for them prepared by Mrs Simpkins, their landlady.

Andrew had a keen interest in birds and in wildlife in general. Harry was an artist; he loved old ruins and sweeping landscapes. This had promised to be the perfect holiday for the two friends.

They had been walking for a couple of hours when Andrew suggested a halt. It was time for sandwiches and a cup of tea from the thermos. They both ate greedily; the fresh air and the chill had served to promote their appetites. They were about to push on in the direction they were heading when their attentions were drawn in separate directions.

'It can't be. Can it?' said Andrew. 'I only caught a glimpse. But if it's what I think it is, one of those birds hasn't been seen in England for at least twenty years.'
'I was just looking at the ruined church. I can't tell what state of disrepair it is in without a closer look. It's definitely medieval though. Who would have thought it, such a fine architectural specimen in the middle of a desolate moor. I must investigate.'

The two men were drawn in opposite directions. Andrew had to look for the bird he had only briefly glimpsed. He wanted to be sure of his identification so he could report the sighting to the ornithological group he belonged to. Harry was equally keen to see the church. Although he did not have to worry about it flying away, he did worry about the amount of daylight left. He estimated that he would require at least a couple of hours to examine it internally and externally to his satisfaction. He was keen to get back to the village whilst it was still light. He had heard many tales, some true and some spurious, regarding the untimely demise of those left on the moor after dusk had descended. The two men agreed to go in their separate directions and to return to the spot where they had enjoyed their luncheon so that they could walk back together.

Harry walked across the moorland towards the church; it was further away than he had estimated and, by the time he arrived at its oak doors, he was feeling very fatigued. City life had not done too much to enhance his physical capacities and a desk job did not prepare him for the vigorous outdoor life. It took all his strength to push the great oak door open. He imagined that the door must have remained fixed in position for many years to cause it to be so stiff. But, on entering the church he found that the candles had been lit and burned brightly in their holders. This was even more surprising as he had not passed any houses or dwellings since leaving the village some hours earlier.

It took his eyes some time to adjust to the candlelight. Recesses of the church remained shrouded in darkness and gloom. He entered and began to walk up the nave. He walked slowly and observed what surrounded him with keen interest. The stained glass window missed a few fragments but would easily be repairable. The pews were covered in a thick layer of dust but did not seem to be suffering from the ravages of damp or decay. Then he noticed the Stations of the Cross adorning the walls. These were covered in dust and festooned with cobwebs. How long must it have been since any devout person followed these he wondered. He himself had not made the devotion since his boyhood. That is when he went to the first station.

All seemed fairly normal until he reached the eleventh station. An ancient priest emerged from the darkness and Harry started in surprise.

'The darkness covers many things,' the priest stated.
'Yes Father.'

‘Do you mind if I join you in your devotion?’
‘Please do.’

As Harry began to recite his prayer the station began to violently dismantle itself. The wood was wrenched away from the plasterwork. A sound like nails flying across a room and the stained glass windows in the opposite wall shattered into a thousand fragments. The priest prayed on and Harry continued because he could see no other course of action. The pews imploded into themselves leaving nothing but matchwood and still the priest prayed and Harry followed suit. Then the giant oak roofing beams began to descend into the transept and the nave. Now Harry was no longer scared, he was terrified. He stopped praying and turned to flee the church fearing for his life, fearing for more than that; but a steely cold grip from a vice-like hand arrested him.

‘Continue your prayer. It is by far the safest course,’ the priest said without relinquishing his grip.

Harry continued his prayer fearful for his safety and wondering what manner of fiend in clerical garb was refusing him a safe exit. As he came to the end of his devotion at the eleventh station a weaker voice spoke to him.

‘Thank you for releasing me.’ It was the priest and as his voice faded, so did the man.

The church had vanished within an instant. Harry looked down and there, in the soft moorland grass, was an old nail.

Harry turned on his heels and rushed to meet Andrew. He covered the distance back to their luncheon spot in half the time it had taken him to walk to the church.

‘It wasn’t what I thought it was,’ said a crestfallen Andrew, ‘it had a spot of yellow where there shouldn’t have been any.’
‘Mine wasn’t what I thought either but it has laid my passion for churches to rest.’ With that Harry fell silent; he would not elaborate further in response to Andrew’s questions and offered no explanation as to why he clutched a rusty old nail.

Escape

Bryn Bartlett

The letter had got to be written, Hilary told himself - it wasn't fair to either of them to go on like this - she was so young, vital, yet her values had the clean-cut-ness of experience. He could even imagine her impatient fury with his present hesitancy - that innate sensitiveness of his that jibbed at hurting anyone . . . least of all *her*. The white paper stared up at him, a small expanse to receive the shattering of their mutual bubble of happiness. He considered the telephone as an alternative, and for the hundredth time dismissed it, that way was even more cruel than the written word, and not nearly so final, involving tears, argument and a bittersweet hell of lovely memory on both sides.

He sighed. It was a curse being a writer, and having a wife like Laura, yet, if he hadn't married her, he might never have discovered he *could* write. When he found the occasional bickering becoming a weekly grouse, that, not-so-gradually developed to a daily moan, he took the line of least resistance, and fled to the blessed solitude of his den. He loathed argument, but Laura, he soon realised, loved it, and her phrase 'But darling, you can't *possibly* mean . . . ' was a danger signal. He learned to side-track with a mild 'perhaps you're right, m'dear' as he made his escape to his latest hobby.

Apparently, she was proud of his sudden swift success as a writer, and apart from the matter of secretaries, never interfered, quite happy in his internment as a literary mollusc, leaving her free to her own varied devices. He often heard her voice that penetrated like a thick honey excusing his invariable absence to personal friends at afternoon tea: 'My husband, he's a writer you know . . . always busy'. In the conversation, he was generally sandwiched between the weather and 'point-to-point's' most recent scandal . . . vile, less vile and disgusting he tabulated shrewdly. He found it simple to have his mid-day meal served on a tray while still at work. Laura managed the servants with an iron hand - they hated but respected her authority, and obviously pitied him. After lunch, he was of the certain opinion he gave his Airedale 'Jasper' a daily romp, but like most dogs, it was Jasper who took his Master out for a breather, while he raced ahead over a common splashed with gold gorse against purple heather in summer, or in winter, scratched at snow until he reached beloved mud. Jasper was a fine dog, but he reached magnificence when he discovered Hope Lawrence painting an autumn woodland scene. After only two prospective sniffs and a friendly pull at a shoe lace, he decided his Master must meet her, and just barked until he arrived, and the chain of lovely memories for both of them began to be forged.

'Darling Hope' . . . how lovely she had looked that day, and what a fool he had felt arriving and expecting to find Jasper stirred to a fury of barking by the swift disappearance of a rabbit's white scut down a dark hole, as so often occurred. Her laughing at the mock anger with the dog, and apologies for her work being interrupted, and all the while that vision of her against the background of carnival trees, dark hair straight and cropped short like a Florentine page, an old emerald green polo sweater, and slacks of rough russet tweed. The grey eyes, level with confidence yet lurking with humour, mouth full, face healthy with outdoor tan, and frankly innocent of cosmetic. He saw again the smudge of paint above the right eyebrow . . . dear darling Hope, that chance meeting had led to *living* again.

Jasper had a new collar that winter. Laura never even noticed. Mah Jongh was the craze that season, and the social round the heaviest ever . . .

And so the saga of Hope and Hilary, not to mention that treasure of a dog, Jasper, began . . .

Hope had rented a cottage in the woods and used it as a studio. They met every afternoon 'by courtesy of Jasper' they coined the phrase, and oft repetition never staled the fun, for, as his name was mentioned the dog would turn and gaze quizzically at them, head cocked to one side, pink tongue lolling, almost a *grin* on his face. It was not only their loving together Hilary reflected, they had shared so much. His stories became enlivened by brilliant illustrations by 'Glee' - Hope's chosen alias for magazine work. When he knew Laura's plans for the evening, he risked staying for dinner, on three occasions (with Laura safely away at someone or other's house party). He'd snatched the Heaven of a weekend. Situations had occasionally arisen reminiscent of a French farce, but their sense of humour saved those luckily rare occurrences becoming tragic. Their complete and utter happiness together was undeniable and rode the breakers of the sea of destiny buoyant as a cork until . . .

The buzzer on the intercom phone went sharply - once - repeated itself like an angry wasp. The elderly man with untidy grey hair sighed and lifted the receiver with resignation . . . a voice like thick honey dripped into the silent room . . . the dog in front of the log fire, yapped as it reached her. 'Henry, I'm tired. Bring Lulu up and come to bed, *now*.' He ventured the meek remonstrance he'd used without effect for 15 years . . . 'I won't be long, m'dear, I'm just -' He got no further. He was engulfed, swept up in the sticky torrent;
'Henry, I've heard that till I'm sick of it . . . you can't possibly . . . '

The pen left his nervous hand, he waited politely for his wife to take a breath, and seized the opportunity with alacrity, 'No, dear, of course not, I'm coming now m'dear.'

Henry gathered his wife's Pekinese in his frail arm, made sure the window was safe against the gale and burglary, ensured the fireguard protected his den from possible conflagration, paused long enough to re-read the last few words of his latest manuscript and muttering 'Rode the breakers of the sea of destiny until', 'I like that, I like that,' turned out the light, softly closed the door, and went slowly upstairs.

It would be a good tale, he reflected, ideal in his customary exquisite translation into French. Thank God, his wife was no linguist.

Henry yawned, Lulu grunted, but whether with pleasure or pain I leave you to judge . . . for we must now take our leave of them as they are at the bedroom door.

A Quiet Summer

Frances M Steel

'Ah, there you are Jilly, I have been looking for you everywhere.' Thomas Lord put a friendly arm around her shoulders. 'I have come to rescue you from the isolated misery of your present existence and bring you back to the warmth of civilisation.'

'If only you could,' sighed Jilly.

'I can, I promise!' It's high time you stopped carrying that torch for Jack! How long is it now? Two years, and you're still living like a nun.' He stopped abruptly, thinking he had gone too far.

'It's okay Tom, I do appear to be a martyr but it's become a way of life now. Mother wrapped me in cotton wool when Jack died. She was so supportive and it went on from there. She coined the phrase 'have a quiet summer dear'.

'You'll have to snap out of it some time Jilly, so now's your chance.'

'Is that what you want to see me about? I thought it was business.'

'Tomorrow Diane and I have a very special friend coming, and as it's your day off we want you to have dinner here at The Country House Hotel. Diane will have to go back on the reception desk and I am on bar duty so we want you to entertain our friend after we have all had a meal together.'

'Are you match making by any chance?'

'As if I would! He's a jolly nice chap, a bachelor, an authority on wild flowers, about our age,' he grinned. Diane, Thomas and Jilly were all at primary school together. 'He's been abroad for years teaching the natives to grow foodstuff or something. He looks after his sister's child. I'm a bit vague about this, he didn't have her in Africa with him. His sister was killed in a plane crash and he is the child's guardian.'

Ah, thought Jilly, could that be the dishy man with a child of about eight she had seen in the foyer last evening. They had given each other interesting glances, she recalled, and the girl with him seemed quite happy. 'Providing Mother doesn't have an attack of the vapours or whatever, I'll come. I appreciate your concern for my welfare, I shall probably be a pain, as I have been out of circulation for so long.'

'Nonsense, I have seen you chatting up the guests from behind the reception desk.'

'All in the course of duty! Nothing personal Sir.' She giggled. She really enjoyed her job.

For reasons she could not explain she omitted to mention next day's plans to her mother, and decided to be out of the house and off to the supermarket in case plans got complicated. There had been some noises in the bathroom quite early but there was no sign of Mother at breakfast, so with a silent prayer to the Almighty, ie 'Please God no vapours today' she left the house.

'Just thought I'd surprise you, dear. I fancied a day in town,' and there she sat, all booted and spurred, ready for the off.

'What on earth gave you the idea I was planning an early start?'

'You had a very cagey look about you last evening. Never underestimate a mother's intuition.'

'In that case, I needn't tell you I am invited back to the hotel this evening for dinner with Thomas and Diane, and I am going to buy a new dress to mark the end of this quiet summer you are always talking about.' There, she had said it.

'I knew it was a mistake to go back to your old job again, Diane always was a bad influence on you, even as long ago as your hockey playing days.'

'You are not referring to the time we went for a cream tea with two spotty youths from the fairground and missed the bus home? Really Mother, you never give up!'

'Mrs Prentigast brought it up in our conversation just last week. She never tires of reminding me that her son married someone quiet.' She shot a meaningful glance at her daughter. Jilly and Henry Prentigast had a little romance for about two months, in their teenage years.

'And I suppose there is a stray male in this party?'

Jilly let that one ride. 'I've just had an idea. I will be having a large dinner tonight so will not be eating at home, so why don't I take you to that new hotel in town. You can 'pig out' and I can have a light snack.'

Mother brightened up at the idea of a nice lunch but clicked her tongue at the vulgar 'pig out' expression. That would be one up on Mrs P, she could boast about the new hotel. Lunch was a great success, and Jilly treated Mother to an 'After Sunshine', the Tia Maria liqueur, that always puts her in a good mood.

'I must tell Mrs Prentigast about 'After Sunshine' Tia Maria. Perhaps her son will treat her to one when he takes her out on her birthday, it really is delicious.'
Harmony restored, shopping for the new dress went like a dream.

Thomas Lord was talking to a tall stranger when Jilly entered the hotel and as it was not the man she expected she kept her distance, but as soon as Thomas saw her he dived over. 'Come and meet Fredrick Steadman, my best mate at college.'
The disappointment must have shown on Jilly's face, and it really bugged her all evening. Conversation never flowed freely. The men got talking about college days and the girls talked hotel business. The man with the child was uppermost in Jilly's mind but she did not mention it.

The hotel waiter came in on cue and the Lords made excuses and left. A couple of teenagers could not have been more tongue-tied as the two strangers at the table racked their brains for something to talk about.

Being very interested in children Jilly ventured, 'Thomas tells me you look after your sister's child, do you see much of her?'
'Ha, Fleur,' the contempt in his voice scathing. 'No, I have never seen her, and I don't want to. She is with foster parents and by the reports I get when I pay the quarterly account, she is her father's child. He left my sister pregnant, an incorrigible womaniser, I would love to come across him, if only to transfer the payments to his account. I do not see why I should pay!'

The cold-hearted outbreak left Jilly speechless and she was about to invent a headache when Diane appeared with two 'Pure Seduction' Tia Maria liqueurs. She winked at Jilly and laughed at Fredrick saying, 'They're called 'Pure Seduction' compliments of the management. Have a nice evening!' She turned and exaggerated a sexy wiggle, tottering on high heels.
'She's a grand girl isn't she?' he enthused. 'Let us go out into the garden with these.'

Now Fredrick was in his element. Every little Scarlet Pimpernel (Anagallis arvensis) to the common Soapwort (Saponaria officinalis), their habitats, Latin names and every detail of rooting etc, went on and on until Jilly could scream.

'I really must go home,' she cut in, and fled into the cloakroom for her coat, and out to her car without saying her goodbyes or thank yous. As she passed her mother's bedroom a loud cough signalled she was still awake and bursting to know what happened.
'No Mother, it was disastrous,' Jilly called out and fled to her own room.

A quick look at the register showed a Mr John Coats and Jane had booked out yesterday. The address was given as Braithwait Farm, which was on the way home for Jilly. Now she remembered a young couple had bought the semi derelict property, Mrs Prentigast had told Mother. They had an eight year old daughter who was boarding at the Convent while they made the place tenable. Oh well, it was a nice dream.

That evening when Jilly got near her car she saw a tall man clutching a teddy bear and looking anxious. It was John Coats. 'You don't know how silly you look,' she giggled.
'Oh yes I do. Can you give me a lift to Braithwait Farm before I get molested, Jane left this behind.'
'Every picture tells a story, what's yours?'
'Better still, what's yours. Does your husband allow you to be out this late?'
'My husband died in a car crash two years ago.'
'I am sorry, I saw your ring and just assumed.'
'Yes, it happens. Does your wife know you go around car parks cuddling a teddy bear?'
'Now you are falling into the same trap. Young Jane is not my child, my sister and brother-in-law have bought Braithwait Farm. Jane is their daughter. I am single, an artist, and am making a studio in one of the barns. I plan to settle here and I will be a serious contender for your company, so any ghosts, real or imaginary, beware. It is so peaceful here. I shall enjoy a quiet summer.'
'In that case I shall invite you home to see my mother.'

Black Deception

Hamish M Davidson

'My glasses, my glasses,' muttered Sybil Grant to herself. 'I've lost my glasses.' She fumbled through her coat pockets - just her purse with her newly acquired pension. Then she tried her handbag. Negative. She remembered putting her new reading glasses back in their case. After that her memory was blank. 'I must be going senile.' She felt like crying. 'The cost of glasses these days, I couldn't afford another pair so soon.'

Sybil had been needing new glasses for some time. Eye strain had brought occasional headaches. But fear of finding glaucoma prevented her from going to an optician. However, her niece, Amy, had finally persuaded her to have her eyes tested. Plucking up courage she went to the optician in the High Street.
'You have nothing to worry about, Mrs Grant,' said the optician. 'Your eyes are quite good for a woman of your age.'
Cheeky devil, thought Sybil. 'Huh, I'm not that old. I'm not seventy 'til next year.'

That was last week. Now her reading glasses were lost. How careless. In her mind she tried to retrace her actions of the past hour.

Today she paid her weekly visit to the library. She was a lady of habit. She would pick one book, go home and start reading it while having her afternoon cup of tea. The library had been closed for three days while some renovations were being carried out. A strong smell of paint greeted her.

'Dear, dear, I hate the smell of new paint. And they've changed the layout of everything. Why can't they leave things the way they are?' she sighed. Putting on her glasses, she browsed through the new thriller section. It was now at the far end of the room. Many American authors and their creations filled one shelf. None of them were of interest to Sybil. She looked along the line of books on a higher shelf following them alphabetically.

'C - c - c. Ah, here we are,' she mumbled to herself. 'Christie, dear Agatha Christie. It's a long time since I read one of her books.' There were several Agatha Christie books on display. Reprints. Up to date copies with up to date jackets. Sybil picked one from the shelf and read the synopsis. It was one she hadn't read and featured her favourite character - Miss Jane Marple. She returned her glasses to their case and put them in her coat pocket. She then handed the book to the assistant at the counter. After the library, she made her way to the post office to collect her pension. Then she phoned her sister in Oxford. Sybil's house phone had been reported out of order.

On leaving the post office, she saw a sinister figure. He was dressed in black leather and a black helmet. Silver chains adorned his jacket. He looked evil, thought Sybil. He must be one of the bikers she had read about in the local paper. They had been causing trouble in the village. She then noticed a Harley Davidson parked at the side of the bank. Slowly she meandered home looking forward to her 'cuppa' and a good read.

It was at this point she realised her spectacles were missing. She was devastated. She was tired and needed her 'cuppa'. She would go home first then decide what to do next.

As she approached the row of cottages several people were working in their gardens or just sitting there soaking up the sun. A dog barked behind her making her turn round. Then she saw him. He was only about twenty yards away. The black figure was following her. He seemed to be eyeing every house as he passed. Sybil remembered the motor cycle at the bank. Was he involved in a bank raid? 'Don't be silly,' she scolded herself. 'You watch too much television.' But then she remembered old Mr Naismith's home had been broken into at the weekend. Was this man the culprit? Who was this evil looking figure? Was he a mugger? Was he a rapist? One reads of such men in the daily newspaper, thought Sybil fretfully. What would Miss Marple do in a situation like this? Sybil knew she was no Miss Marple. She now felt uneasy. Not exactly in keeping with the lady sleuth from St Mary Mead. She turned round again. He seemed much closer. If only she could run. Run? That was a laugh. With her arthritic knee she could hardly walk. However, she did manage to quicken her step a little, wincing at the pain.

Two minutes later she was opening her door with a trembling hand. Once inside, she took off her coat and hung it up. At that moment there was a ring on the doorbell. Sybil hesitated then opened the door slowly. She froze. Her heart almost missed a beat. It was him. The black menacing figure was standing on her doorstep. He at once removed his helmet and unzipped the top of his jacket, revealing a clerical collar. 'A clergyman,' cried Sybil in a soft voice. He had a broad smile and his eyes seemed friendly.

'Um - Mrs Grant?'
'Y-y-yes,' she replied nervously.
'Sorry if I startled you. I'm the new vicar of St Judes. I was in the phone box at the post office, when I noticed your spectacle case on the shelf. Fortunately your name and address were written on the case.'

Sybil remembered she had to use her glasses in the phone box while checking her sister's new number. She closed her eyes with relief. 'Oh, thank you, vicar. Thank you. It was very kind of you. When I saw you following me, I - I - '
'I'm sorry if I frightened you. As you see I run a motor cycle. I prefer it to a car. I enjoy the freedom of the bike.'

Sybil Grant now felt relaxed, so she asked the vicar in for afternoon tea. 'That is the least I can do.'

For half an hour they shared a pot of tea and some home-made scones in the front room. He seems such a nice young man, thought Sybil. As for Miss Marple - she'll have to wait.

The Curse

M F Base

I have always been a little wary of DIY activities and consider them as over-rated and usually expensive past times! Efforts to convince our female partners of these facts is usually a pretty futile exercise even when you mention that the old bank balance will suffer a bit!

Unfortunately for us males, the female species and more particularly the house-proud married variety, see spring from their point of view! For it is a heaven sent opportunity to get the males out of their comfortable chairs and once again resurrect that indigenous female curse called spring cleaning! A curse which seems to pass from generation to generation world without end!

It starts quite innocently of course in the dying days of winter (though it is difficult to say when that is exactly) usually with the odd hint or remark directed at the unsuspecting male and which he will do well not to ignore completely! Smile if it kills you when you are told that 'The paper in the dining room is beginning to look a bit grubby' or 'I think it's about time we did something about that ceiling in the spare room'! It's all part of what would seem to be their pre-determined demoralisation exercise and together with other blatant warning signs, which, as the weeks pass without much action, might tend to create a false sense of security plus a faint hope that it might be nothing to worry about! Fat chance!

Before long the blow falls with a casual remark from 'Her who must be obeyed' to the effect that 'As you have a few days' holiday coming up next week I think it might be a good idea if we started to think about 'spring cleaning' (I like that bit!). This or something very similar starts the whole dreary process off and before you realise what has happened you can find yourself fully embroiled in a situation where the furniture starts to move around and the air is filled with the noise of washing machines and vacuum cleaners working overtime!

With that in mind you can decide to operate a 'waste not - want not' process and make some effort (if only in spirit) to effect a small cost saving! Usually this entails a visit to the garden shed and/or loft to carry out a somewhat half-hearted search for ladders, steps, scrapers and similar tools, some dried up brushes you thought you had somewhere, pots of now semi-solid paints, plus anything that might prove useful and save a few pence!

It's all a complete waste of time and energy really particularly when you consider that a fair proportion of all the available DIY currency this year will merely be spent on creating yet more redundancies which will end up inevitably adding to those already cluttering up the shed and/or loft!

However though you are by now hopelessly committed, it's as well to apply an element of caution before you finally trundle off the local DIY Emporium! Be sure to leave the choice of paint colours, wallpaper patterns etc required for the decor, strictly to 'Her indoors' and thereby considerably reduce the trauma of the whole operation! To carry out this task alone and without consultation is to invite disaster and will invariably bring forth such comments as 'This paper is more suitable for papering the coalhouse' or 'That isn't quite the colour I visualised for the bedroom' plus other perhaps more pungent remarks delivered with that 'What did I marry this fool for' look!

But everything has to end sometime and finally comes the dawn of the day when the last strip of wallpaper is hung and the last paint brush is laid to rest and when hopefully, you can relax and think of something more useful to do! Don't however expect a 'well done' pat on the back for all your efforts, instead it is more likely to be that well known and frustrating 'Oh look you have spilt a drop of paint on my new carpet' syndrome and which one must, for the sake of matrimonial harmony take with a smile while at the same time suppressing all thoughts of mayhem and homicide!

So while I search for the white spirit in order to remove that imagined spot on the carpet at the same time swearing about the weather which now that all is complete, has decided to relent into warmth and sunshine, please spare a thought for those martyrs to that awful 'curse'!

While young and newly wed you can be enthusiastic about these 'spring cleaning' capers, treating them as all part of the 'fun' but as the years pass and old age creeps on that enthusiasm becomes somewhat tempered by a little wisdom and equanimity which combined with creaking bones and muscles provide excellent reasons why the usual leap into such activities should be taken only after a great more thought and care! After all there are better ways of earning a living!

X-Ray Terror

Lucinda Hayes-Rowe

Anxiously I parked my car and checked my letter and directions to the Breast Screening Unit. Walking towards reception I thought, 'Oh well, here goes - never had a mammogram before - told it hurts too!' I was duly X-rayed and engaged in jovial conversation.

The pleasant lady Radiographer said, 'Just drop your shoulders and try to keep very still, will you? I know it hurts a little but it doesn't take long. We'll start with the left breast.'

Jokingly, I replied 'Gosh you must see all shapes and sizes, is it easier X-raying if you've a size 32 bust?'

The reply was, 'Well, surprisingly, not really, just a couple more shots now and that's it.'

I recall thinking that technology is marvellous these days and that it would be just a routine X-ray every three years.

I continued in daily life. Working, writing, shopping, working out at the gym, practising yoga positions, reading and usually with my dear cat Henry, nearby. My teenage daughters were enjoying good end-of-term results and Nick, my husband, revelled in his latest business launch. Life ticked along beautifully.

Six days later I received a follow-up letter from another hospital informing me that they were not satisfied with the results of my mammogram and this threw me into instant panic. I telephoned my friend, Anna.

'Oh Anna, I'm so desperately scared - I know there's something wrong - they wouldn't call me back so quickly otherwise.' Anna enquired if I'd told the family, but of course I hadn't dared to worry them.

'No, of course I haven't, they are on a real high - it's the school play soon, Nick is obviously very concerned.' Later I gathered myself together and told myself I'd got cancer, and as my mum died of it, it had to be in the genes.

I'll never know how I got through the next few days. Simply by throwing myself into projects - gardening, writing, walking and eating. Also, having been on HRT for five years and knowing its possible breast cancer risks, I threw them instantly in the bin as they were poison. It was to be Evening Primrose from now on.

Darkening thoughts came upon me. 'Reconstruction, chemotherapy, hair falling out, hell, what a fate! I know, however, they can do wonders. Karen, a close friend had had a full implant and she's never looked back. She never told a soul until she threw a *new boobs launch party'*.

I then mused, 'Oh well, look on the bright side, girl - could end up with a size 32A for a change. Hell, what if . . . oh God.' Suddenly it dawned on me and I felt my left breast to check if there was any pain. Henry was curled up on a nearby chair. He sensed I was in distress and I stroked him, thanking him for always being there for me. Afterwards I sat in a yoga lotus position to meditate.

I pretended I was on a desert island in warm sunshine and the sea was lapping around my feet - I felt only good things - I had no pain and I would conquer my illness. I had inner peace. My husband and family were all wonderful and I was in total control of my fate.

After the yoga session I wandered from room to room, then made a huge sandwich, and proceeded to binge. 'Well,' I thought, 'some turn to drink, others smoke - me, well - food I guess.'

I engaged in mammoth reading sessions at the library, anything at all on breast cancer. Inner panic was now deeply rooted, however, externally, for the sake of my family I had to stay calm. The eating binges continued as did the yoga. Gradually the appointment for the scan arrived. Nick, my husband came with me for support. As I was called the nurse said, 'We are sorry to have to recall you, just routine but I'm sure you have been so anxious.'

'That,' I replied, is an understatement.'

'Anyway, we'll have you all sorted and the doctor will explain. I'll arrange for a cup of tea for when we've finished the scans.' The nurse was very pleasant and I recall thinking that they must see some pretty sad cases with breast cancer. Outside, Nick comforted me after my ordeal. I relayed the appointment to him.

I tried to remain calm. 'They've found an area that they refer to as a glandular erosion - I saw it clearly on the screen, very scary - big white area showing . . . I have to have a biopsy. It's OK, I know my fate. I have cancer.'

Nick hugged me tight 'Oh darling - no! Look, they are doing all they can and acting very quickly. Anyway, most types are treatable, science has advanced so much - remember Margaret? She's fine now.'

My swift reply was, 'I have to wait two bloody days too for the biopsy and at another hospital with specialist equipment. I'm now really scared - in fact petrified. Not for me - for you and the girls. My only wish is to see them grow up, go to University and have a good life. Hell, I'm only 50 for God's sake!' Nick was totally supportive and tried to reassure me that it was all a routine procedure.

I then pleaded with him. 'Only a few friends know. Let's keep it that way. And if you don't mind - let's drop all reference to this till the results are back. I'm just sinking into projects - and if you haven't noticed I'm on an eating binge too!'

'Fine,' replied Nick, 'anyway how about Angelo's, Saturday night, we'll binge, OK?'

My immediate friends sent cards and letters, a bouquet from Anita, Anna, flowers too from Lisa and a beautiful crystal necklace from Lin, Lisa's mum, a jewellery designer. Throughout, my family continued their routine, and I found inner peace in yoga. I certainly went on a binge and put on 6lbs knowing, of course, that once my fate was diagnosed I could lose the weight.

The biopsy was duly taken. The doctor reassured me that she was sure that I would be fine but had to take the necessary precautions and that it would be a further four days before the results would be available.

On arrival home, Anna telephoned. I jokingly told her I fancied a 32C bust like her. Of course she craves a 36B, but then one's never happy with their lot. That night I had a terrible dream. I was in hospital having undergone breast surgery. I was so distressed and immediately felt my breasts to check they were still there. Hell - pure living hell. What a nightmare dream and so real.

I was so frightened but I couldn't show my terror to the family. At least I knew my fate! My inner thoughts were of my mum. She must have gone through hell and back and she never told us how ill she was. We last saw her alive on our wedding day, seventeen years ago. She wanted us to go ahead with the wedding, never, ever, did I think that she would be too ill to attend. God rest her soul. Diagnosed and dead within three months aged only fifty-four.

I found true comfort with my cat on restless nights. On parading back and forth from the bathroom, I would eventually curl up with him on the sofa. He was a real salvation. The time between the initial X-ray to final diagnosis seemed an eternity.

The first breast screening was taken at a mobile screening unit in Worcester Royal Infirmary, the second follow-up ultrasound scan at The Princess of Wales Hospital at Bromsgrove, while the biopsy taken at the Alexandra Hospital at Redditch. The final diagnosis was given back at the Princess of Wales hospital at Bromsgrove. All this travelling between hospitals in three different towns of course made for even more anxiety.

Daily life was becoming increasingly difficult to get through. I recall pushing a trolley along in the supermarket, having a shopping list but gazing into space. I would look at toddlers in trolleys, ladies chatting and people frantically shopping. I would pick up items then put them back in a vacant gaze. Once I created a scene when items fell from a shelf. I tearfully said, 'Oh - look I'm really sorry, I'm just not feeling well and I can't bend down to help as I've such a splitting headache.'

Inner thoughts were thumping inside my head. That evening my daughters were full of stories of their day. I had to appear interested although having a severe headache.

'And guess what?' said Clare. 'I'm the cross-country captain for this term, can't wait for Friday - the course is really boggy and someone's bound to fall in the brook.'

'Err - yuk,' replied Amy, 'you better not be near me.'

The girls told me that I was looking rather faded and disinterested. 'Hey Mum - you OK? Anything wrong? Bad work day hey?'

'No,' I replied, 'just a really bad headache. I may have an early night.'

They both cuddled me lovingly and Henry too jumped on me for some fuss.

On the night before the final appointment I was incapable of sleeping. My only thoughts were 'If only I could turn on time.' The appointment wasn't until 1.30pm. I had to go downstairs as I was keeping Nick awake. I knew if I did some yoga I may be able to relax a little. Nick comforted me and I said, 'Look, in the morning make no reference to the day OK? - the girls will be up ready for school - I'll take them then go to work. Be back here for 12.30. They're already asking questions about the sudden 'good wishes', and 'thinking of you' cards, not to mention the flowers. I had to pass it off by saying I have interest in articles for publication.

He said he loved me and would stand by me whatever.

D-Day finally came. Nick drove the nine drawn-out miles of the motorway and I gazed over a gardening magazine and nervously chatted making no reference to my impending doom.

'Yeah, I think we should go for that large blue pot for the courtyard - fancy a clematis or something in it?' I stated.

'Why not?' said Nick, 'we'll stop off and buy it as a treat on the way back.'

'Well that depends,' I answered in a shaky tone. Inner panic was setting fast. We drew up outside reception and Nick put a comforting hand on my arm.

On checking in, we were the only people there.

'Oh God - I really can't take any more of this waiting - I'll crack before I get along that corridor.' I felt quite physically sick with the mental torture. I rested my head on Nick's shoulder. I had come this far and I couldn't break down yet.

'Darling - we'll be fine - I'm with you - whatever . . .'

'Oh Nick, I'm so scared - I'd do anything other than face Dr Evans.'

I'm feeling empty inside and full of anxiety. I've even got heart palpitations. I just want the results 'I can't take anymore,' I mumbled.

As Nick hugged me close, Dr Evans arrived and smiled at me. 'Mrs Hayes-Rowe, would you care to step this way? Were you able to park - it seems very busy today?

In a trembly voice I replied 'Yes, thank you.'

I will never forget the words the doctor uttered and I could have kissed her when she informed me that the test was benign and that my condition would just go away. There was no cause for worry. I broke down and wept uncontrollably. Nick just buried his head in his hand and then relayed how brave I'd been throughout and how proud he was of me.

Outside we threw our arms around one another. 'Oh Nick - this has to be better than winning the lottery.' He agreed. You simply can't put a price on good health. I was still shaking for some time afterwards.

We commemorated that special day with lunch at the garden centre and buying a rose bush. In all, I couldn't have got by without family friends and the wonderful support. I suddenly felt very humble thinking some have to go it all alone with no one to turn to.

It was all as a bad dream and I was totally prepared for being told I'd breast cancer. I am still in awe of my reprieve - I value most things now in a very different way and I live life to the full. It was as though I'd lost three weeks of my life and could have slept for a week. I was utterly exhausted to the core.

Since that day I've pulled myself back in line and lost the weight I put on. I recently had the opportunity of competing in the Race for Life organised by Cancer Research and I walked in temperatures of 33°C, proudly displaying my memory banner with 'Mum' written on it. The walk was one of immense satisfaction. Not only did I complete two laps in soaring temperatures but I also raised a total of £123 for Cancer Research. This is to be an annual event and next time I know that I will be walking and recalling the pain and anguish I suffered, but thanking God I have at least been spared.

A Statue To Memory

Clive Cornwall

One warm summer evening I sat with my uncle Willett in the orchard behind his little place. We drank a couple of ales and he as he often did, told me one of his many World War II tales. It would seem that some thirty or so young girls arrived in Natley St James on a hot summer's day, the tar sticking to the soles of their shoes, they were carrying an assortment of boxes, bundles and cases. They were from London, mostly the East End.

'Don't see the bleedin' picture house.'

They were a strange mixture of loud talk and silent apprehension.

'Tit, look at that cow.'

The cow was a bull. Their arrival had no official welcoming party, but from behind each set of net curtains, they were both seen and assessed.

'Bloody hell, I can smell the Devil's armpits.' Bonnie was the loudest one of the bunch and her use of language was very free. They had yet to get used to the odours of the countryside, they were to be at Woodside Farm housed in a hut which was situated beneath chestnut trees. This was a strange and alien environment for them. The nearest most of them had been to rural life was Regent's Park.

'Bloody spooky,' bellowed Bonnie as she got ready for bed. 'Make sure you lock that damned door. Anything can happen in these places.'

'Wonder if they'll cop it again tonight?' They were thinking of London and their families. In fact London 'copped it' most nights as the distant red glow confirmed.

The nightly bombing of London and the resultant red glow could be seen from Natley St James quite clearly.

The girls were working on local farms doing jobs they never knew existed. They were quick to learn. They were to learn even quicker when a detachment of Canadian troops moved into neighbouring huts for a short while. The word 'manoeuvres' took on quite a new meaning for the girls. 'Maple leaf wonders' one of the girls called them. Even a dance of sorts was organised with a wind-up gramophone and 78's Chuck's mouth organ was pressed into service too. He sat on an upturned oil drum with 'Skinny Liz's' bra stretched over his head, like two ear muffs. Promises that were not meant to be kept were made. Early one morning the girls got up to find the young men gone.

Ashes of the campfire from the night before lay dying and close by an upturned oil drum.

Bonnie the loud couldn't care less. The girl stood alone and wept and wept. The ashes and the oil drum and all about was but a statue to memory.

A Little Cottage In Sussex

J Howling Smith

The car was hot on that August day, we decided to stop on the winding country road near a public footpath sign. After securing the car and feeling the gentle breezes caressing our brows we started to walk in single file along that inviting unknown way, not a word was spoken between us, just thoroughly enjoying and absorbing (if you can) the utter peace of our surroundings. We walked for about a mile when we came to a fork in the path, on the right was a Private sign but on the left was a very much used cart track, now ridged by tractor wheels and hardened by the relentless sun of the exceptional summer we were experiencing, we looked at each other and nodded in agreement that we would go left.

The sublime atmosphere was as a magnet to us both, we picked our way just with the united kind of communication of nod or look, no word was spoken.

On each side of us now were grain fields almost ready for harvesting, wheat on one side and barley on the other. John lightly touched me on the shoulder and with a finger, as I turned, pointed to a tiny field mouse tucking into a luscious wheat head. It was so small and its coat was so shiny, it was only about two feet away from us, our presence did not seem to worry it at all, then, as we watched, the tiny creature was gone in a flash.

As we walked on John spotted a magpie closely followed by its mate, several sky larks flew up as if from nowhere at the sound of our approach. A pheasant strutted across the pathway in front of us, he did not seem to mind us at all. In fact he kind of sized us up before disappearing through the hedge. Ah, I thought, this is far better than any television. John seemed to read my thoughts as he said, 'This beats anything you have to pay a licence for.'

At that moment we were both conscious of a rich, wonderful smell and as we walked on, it got stronger and stronger. We looked at each other and said together 'Raspberry jam' and smiled. As we went on the smell was really getting to us. Soon we came to a little wicket gate which was half open, it was painted white and although it was obviously very old, was in tip top condition due to much loving care. The half open entry was so inviting we found ourselves stopping and slowly turning in. The pathway was cobbled, no sign of a weed anywhere. Edged by herbaceous borders with, it seemed, all of my childhood memories flying back at me of my father's pre-war garden. At the back were hollyhocks, sunflowers, golden rod, delphiniums, hare bells, foxgloves, antirrhinums, graduating down to nasturtiums, pansies and birdseye.

We stealthily went in and both felt that we were taking a great liberty, it was so peaceful we were drawn on till we came to where the garden opened out, a large lawn which, although it seemed to grow just where it wanted to, was well mown and very green. In the corner of the garden stood a gnarled old apple tree absolutely laden with fruit, a large black dog was asleep on his back under the tree. He just about opened one eye and gave half a wag of his tail then turned right over as if he was approving of our entry. A hand-made wooden seat was also under the tree, again that too was aged and well cared for.

The door to the beautiful cottage was half open too, we could see the polished oak beams gleaming in the hallway, it looked so inviting, the little latticed windows sparkled, the gentle breezes causing the pretty summer curtains to move gently.

We were just about to go and retrace our steps when a friendly voice called 'Hello there folks, would you like a seat for a while?' A very elderly gentleman using a stick came from the side of the house, he had a wonderful smile and I could not help but notice he had, in spite of his obvious age, most of his own teeth. He was weather-beaten and had a crop of thick white hair. We went forward and shook his hand, apologised, and introduced ourselves. We said we were enticed in by the delicious smell of the raspberry jam and the delightful garden. He was Jack, Jack Greenall and he called to his wife Elsie, she came bustling out drying her hands on a spotless white tea towel. She was a chubby person with her grey hair pinned neatly into a bun, her face was rosy and cheery. We explained as we had to Jack, the reason why we were in their garden. She smiled, a satisfied smile and asked us if we would stay and have a cup of tea.

The house was very cool, the furniture was oak and it showed the years of care that had been bestowed on it. Everywhere was immaculate, the surround of the fireplace was also oak with a little antique clock in the centre. At one end a picture in a gilt frame of a young man in uniform, they told us that he, David, had died during the war at the age of 19. They had another son, he was called Jimmy, he lived in London, he had married a lovely girl called Carol. They had blessed them with two beautiful grandchildren, a girl named Rosie, aged 10, and a little boy named Peter, aged 5. They went on to say that Carol was just like a daughter to them, they all came to visit on the first Sunday in every month, no matter what the weather.

The tea duly arrived in china cups (I suspect they were bought out especially) and a plate of buns. 'I always have to make these today, she said, 'because the family are coming to visit tomorrow and young Peter always asks for one of Gran's buns.'
The chatter was so pleasant, the room just spelt out peace and tranquillity, I could not help feeling a little envious over the fact that they had so much that does not need lots of money to acquire. So many people of today strive so hard for vanity and as they get all they want they still are not happy and go on striving for more and more. There was a deep understanding and affection between Jack and Elsie, in this modern world those two qualities are rare in people.

We stayed for nearly three hours and were duly presented with a pot of that delicious raspberry jam which John left money for in the bathroom, because he knew that they would be very offended if we had tried to offer it. We were reluctant to go and I found myself giving them a really genuine hug and kiss. They told us not to forget them and if ever we were in that area at any time we would be so welcome. We did not walk back in single file, we both felt the need for that special nearness that radiated from that little cottage in Sussex.

THE POTTERY PIG

Janice Turner

Madeleine fingered her wedding ring nervously as she waited for her daughter, Justine, to emerge from the small changing room in 'Beau Brides', a select establishment in the High Street.

Madeleine's sister, Frances, bought her wedding dress from there ten years ago, when she married Martin - boyish Martin who fell head over heels with elegant and witty Frances, who made heads turn with her flame-red hair and fine bone structure. Men literally fell at her feet, she dated plenty, but none seemed to fit the bill until Martin came along. At twenty-six, he was eight years her junior, and he suited Frances perfectly, because Martin always gave her whatever she wanted.

Even when they were growing up, thought Madeleine, Frances was always the selfish one - and the prettiest. Not that Madeleine minded, she was more of a tomboy, climbing trees and playing conkers with James Crossley, the naughtiest boy in their school. If Frances wanted to borrow any of Madeleine's clothes, she didn't care. Madeleine preferred to wear trousers and a T-shirt, while Frances always dressed in frilly, fussy things. She spent hours at the mirror in her bedroom, pretending to be one of the models in the 'Softer Skin' commercial on TV. Even when her mother called her to help with the washing up, Frances always pretended not to hear, which left Madeleine nearly every night, with her elbows plunged deep in soapsuds. The funny thing was, Frances always managed to get away with it, perhaps because she was the youngest - Daddy's girl, his 'Francie'.

He never called me 'Maddy', Madeleine thought ruefully. She was then gangly and awkward, with freckles and a brace on her teeth. Frances seemed to bypass the usual childhood embarrassments, and always appeared as though she was a contender for a photo shoot, with perfect skin, shiny hair and a smile which could captivate Medusa.

As Madeleine sat patiently in 'Beau Brides', she smiled wryly to herself, remembering the time when she won a prize for pottery at Elmhurst Secondary. How Frances envied her moment of glory! Momentarily wishing that Mr Lowe hadn't barred her from his extracurricular pottery class; for having 'incisor-like fingernails', as he so aptly put it.

Frances had flounced out of the classroom with that certain air which was so characteristically hers, leaving Madeleine feeling rather ashamed of her 'little sister', though there was only two years between them.

Madeleine had won a five pounds Boots voucher for her pottery pig. Mr Lowe had said it was an 'imaginative and decorative work of art'. Its little body was painted with primroses and tulips. It even had a ring through its nose which added to its charm. From that day, Madeleine treated it like a talisman, it got her through her 'A' levels, then university. It had travelled with her to her first job interview at the Agricultural College three miles from town, where she applied to work as a Laboratory Technician, its little ringed nose, peeping out of the side pocket of her handbag. She got the post, of course, and worked long and hard before falling in love and marrying Jim, who years before had pulled at her plaits and chased her round the playground with a handful of worms.

Frances was the chief bridesmaid at her wedding, doing it under pressure, as she hated the colour that Madeleine had picked for her dress. On all the wedding photographs, Frances could be seen scowling. Even at twenty-two, Frances behaved like a spoilt child, whenever she couldn't get her own way. Like the time when she 'accidentally' broke Madeleine's pottery pig in the middle of one of her many tantrums.

The argument had nothing to do with Madeleine, but her pig was the nearest object to hand, and it fell to the wooden parquet floor of the living room with a crash and broke in half. But what was worse, the pig's golden nose ring which gave him a character of his own, buckled and snapped off, leaving the little creature with a forlorn expression.

Madeleine never forgave Frances for this particular misdemeanour. Even when she tried to seduce Jim from under her nose when they were dating, she put it down to 'sisterly jealousy', and felt a huge sigh of relief when, in the end, she caught Martin Amory's eye, (albeit many years and boyfriends later) over the frozen pizzas in the supermarket. He was, at that time, an up and coming accountant with a weakness for beautiful things. His house was full of antiques and exotic drapes.

Frances' sleek good looks and impeccable style enchanted him, and in no time at all, the Reverend Collins was reading their banns from the pulpit at St Saviours. Their wedding was a big affair. Martin's family were rich business people who had invested thousands in stocks and shares, they paid for the lot.

Madeleine was not invited to accompany Frances up the aisle, she preferred Martin's three cute nieces who wore dresses of rose pink, their coronets of apple blossom fitting snugly on their blonde bobbed heads, while Frances stole the show in an extravagant ivory satin creation which was the most expensive dress that 'Beau Brides' had to offer. They honeymooned in the Seychelles, and returned ten days later, to Martin's neat semi, to live a life of marital bliss.

The bubble burst, it lasted as long as Madeleine had expected. Seven years and two months later, Frances flounced out of her childless marriage into the arms of Lorenzo Gattini, an industrialist from Ravenna, who had business dealings with the Amory family, though far more affluent. Even the Amory coffers were not large enough to provide Frances with the luxury she felt was her right.

With each year of her marriage, Frances wanted more until, in the end, unhappy with her lot, she fluttered her eyelashes at Lorenzo and, that was that, he was smitten. Madeleine could not believe the heartless way Frances had treated kind and tolerant Martin, who had pleaded with her not to leave him, but she was already seduced by Lorenzo's lifestyle and a dejected Martin eventually received Frances' wedding ring through the post together with a curt message of rejection. He suddenly realised that beauty is very much only skin deep. A divorce was inevitable 'That nearly killed Dad . . . and Martin', Madeleine mused noting too, how the phone calls from Italy had become very few and far between.

As Madeleine was just thinking how lucky Martin was, now that he had at last found the bride of his dreams, the door of the changing room snapped open, bringing a swift end to Madeleine's reverie of past times. Justine looked beautiful in her simply cut dress, and wore a tasteful velvet bow at the back of her head. How lovely of her, Madeleine thought, to have introduced her bubbly friend, Patricia, who shared her passion for riding, to a doleful Martin, who desperately needed someone to fill his life.

Patricia emerged from behind Justine. She was as plain as a piece of paper, but she looked radiant in her stunning cream wedding dress and veil . . .

Many years later, Justine Foster was cleaning her lounge one bright morning, she knew she had to be careful as she flipped her feather duster over her late mother's pottery pig, as it had a crack round its middle where it had been mended by her grandfather long before she was born. Her mother had told her the story many times and of how Martin had produced the one item which re-created the charm and character of the little creature.

Justine placed the pig lovingly back on the sideboard, and its little golden nose ring sparkled and shone in the June sunshine.

ALTER EGO

Kim Huggens

'You didn't!'

'Oh, I did. And it was good . . . ' Kiera mused, smiling slyly into her vodka and coke.

'But that is so bitchy, Kiera!' Eden cried incredulously, rocking forward on her bar stool, excited.

'But I didn't have to do anything,' Kiera boasted proudly, nonchalantly examining her perfectly manicured nails. 'He made all the moves.'

Eden stared at her best friend with new respect. 'He's married for crying out loud!' she shouted, throwing her arms wildly around her head. 'You're just too dizzy to realise what you could have done to his poor wife. I mean she . . . '

'He wouldn't have come to me if he loved her,' Kiera abruptly interrupted. 'He obviously wasn't getting it from her, so . . . ' She shrugged carelessly and took another sip of her drink.

Eden considered this for a while. Her strapless dress was gradually slipping down her chest, so she hastily dragged it back to its original position, and guiltily looked around her to see if anyone had noticed.

'You should've got a smaller one,' Kiera nodded past her glass towards the denim garment.

'Yeah,' Eden agreed. Damn someone *had* noticed. She laughed nervously. 'Well, I've lost quite a bit of weight since I bought it.'

'So buy something new!' Kiera remarked, rummaging through her handbag for her cigarettes and a lighter which actually worked.

'I would if I had the money,' Eden explained, 'but the office gives us such crap pay, it's unbelievable.'

'Tell me about it,' Kiera groaned, delving deeper into her bag. She found a packet of cigarettes, but the four lighters she had discovered were all empty. She sighed. 'Been trying to give it up anyway,' she said, before returning the battered packet to its hiding place, along with the other remnants of previous bad habits. 'Rent's due soon, and I've hardly got anythin',' she complained.

'I know. Oh, by the way - are you going to the office party?' Eden asked.

Kiera rolled her eyes. 'No way. *She's* gonna be there.'

'She?'

'His wife.'
'So? Of course she is - you work with her! She doesn't know, does she?'
'I'm not gonna take any chances, Eden,' Kiera argued. 'I mean, if she knows, she might do something.'
'I hardly think this guy's gonna tell his wife that he's been sleeping with you, is he?' Eden replied.
Kiera looked at her aggressively.
'I know, but it'll be really difficult being in the same room as her, y'know?'
'But you're in the same room as her *every day!'* Eden cried.
'Yeah, I suppose so,' Kiera agreed, admitting her defeat. She laughed, and gulped down the rest of her vodka and coke. Putting her coat on, she straightened the straps, and stood up. 'C'mon, we'd better get back.' She fished in her pockets for her car keys.
Eden left the rest of her orange juice, and snatched the keys off Kiera. 'Nah, mate, *I* drive,' she said, walking out of the pub before Kiera could protest.

'Merry Christmas everybody!' Santa Claus drunkenly shouted. Kiera gazed around the large room she had just entered. The crew of the Jolly Roger were hanging around the drinks table, and in one corner of the room, a nun was showing more leg than Kiera thought possible to have. Lady Godiva was busy flirting with the frilled lizard, and Clint Eastwood was attempting to break dance. All around her, characters from films, television, mythology . . . animals, aliens and pieces of fruit, danced, chatted and flirted. Eden bumped into her.
'Fancy dress was a good idea!' she commented, putting the visor down on her Darth Vader helmet.
'I suppose,' Kiera agreed. The astronaut costume was hot and heavy. She would *die* for a classic little Gucci number right now.
'I'm gonna go and find Nick,' Eden added, winking, before disappearing in the colourful crowd.
'He's the one dressed up as Captain Hook!' Kiera called after her, suddenly feeling very conspicuous. She hastily made her way to the toilets, and wriggled out of her restricting costume. Looking at her reflection in the mirror, she wondered what she could be. All she was wearing were white pedal pushers and a pink shirt. Glancing around for ideas, she spotted the large supplies of toilet roll on the shelves.

Wrapping the tissue round her in endless reams, she decided an Egyptian mummy would be good enough for the night. Just as she was running out of loo roll, Eden waltzed in. Taking her helmet off, she shook her hair out of her face. She took one look at Kiera and burst into manic laughter. 'What the hell are you doing?' she cried, pointing at the horrible mess.

'There is no way I'm gonna wear *that* all night!' she replied, nodding towards the crumpled astronaut.

'Swap then?' Eden offered, grinning broadly.

'What?' Kiera asked, shocked. 'You wanna wear *that* thing?'

'If it'll persuade you not to look a prat.'

Kiera considered the offer. 'Go on then,' she agreed, unwrapping the tangled mess from around her body. 'I like Darth Vader anyway,' she added hastily jumping into the suit.

'The astronaut is more my size,' Eden commented, turning round to see the back of the costume in the mirror. When Kiera was ready, Eden opened the door. 'Come on then, we'd better get back in there before we miss all the juicy gossip.'

'Did you find Nick?' Kiera asked.

'Yeah, he's waiting with my drink over at a table,' Eden explained. She waved to Captain Hook who smiled back. 'See you later,' she added.

'Hey, Eden!' Kiera shouted. She turned around. 'Use the Force!' she shouted, laughing. When Eden had returned to her seat, Kiera decided to try and find somebody to talk to. The vicar looked promising . . .

The angel scanned the room, her eyes carefully piercing the crowd in her search . . . walking deeper into the party, she felt in her pocket to check the knife was still safely secured out of sight . . .

'You were Darth Vader a minute ago!' Nick exclaimed, as Eden sat down next to him.

'I swapped with Kiera,' Eden replied.

'Well, the astronaut suits you,' Nick complimented, before pulling her up to the dance floor.

'I can't dance!' Eden cried, embarrassed.

'Neither can I,' Nick shrugged, smiling sweetly . . .

An angel walked purposefully towards an astronaut, her right hand slowly moving to her pocket. As she neared her target, she reached for the knife, pulling it abruptly from its hiding place and raising it threateningly. But Captain Hook noticed. His eyes widened with fear, and he let out an awful scream.

'She's got a knife!' The cry echoed around the room, and the astronaut turned around. As the knife came down, an arm shot up, both making sickening contact in the middle. The astronaut screamed in pain, and Captain Hook stood shocked, holding the blood-soaked arm. Darth Vader came running over, swearing and cursing.

'Oh my God! I knew you'd try something, but not this!' she cried, taking off her helmet to look at the wound more closely.

Sarah, the angel, stared in pure horror at Kiera. 'You're not an astronaut!' she exclaimed incredulously.

'Well done!' Kiera shouted back sarcastically. 'How could you do this?'

'You slept with my husband,' Sarah growled fiercely. 'I've got two kids at home who want to know why Daddy doesn't love Mummy any more!' she seethed, her teeth clenched as the tears rolled down her cheeks. The knife lay on the floor, its cruel blade reddened and glistening. Tears mingled with blood and wine, as Eden collapsed to her knees, the pain running through her body in a non-stop flow. Elvis Presley had dialled nine, nine, nine, and Kiera clenched her hand around the deep wound. Santa Claus came running over with the first aid kit, seeming surprisingly sober, but by the time he had reached the wound, Eden's eyes had grown hazy, her breathing erratic, and she passed out, her arm falling limp in Kiera's grasp.